Handmade

Holiday

Homicide

A Kiki Lowenstein Mystery
(Book #10)

Joanna Campbell Slan

Author's Note:
In the chronology of Kiki's life, this book comes after
Killer, Paper, Cut (Book #9) and before ***Shotgun,***
Wedding, Bells (Book #11). For a complete list of all Kiki's
adventures, go to **www.JoannaSlan.com** or to
http://tinyurl.com/JoannaSlan
<<<<<<<<<<◇>>>>>>>>>>

Handmade, Holiday, Homicide: A Kiki Lowenstein Scrap-
n-Craft Mystery (Book #10)

Published by Spot On Publishing, Inc., 9307 SE Olympus
Street, Hobe Sound FL 33455

Cover Credit: Jessica Compton | www.jessiecompton.com
Interior Book Format and Back Cover: The Killion
Group | The KillionGroupInc.com
Photo Credits: Pei Ling Hoo | Dreamstime.com -
Christmas Stars Wrapping Paper; Udra1 | Dreamstime.com
– Christmas Sheet of Paper and Baubles; Kitchner Bain |
Dreamstime.com – Christmas Wrapping; Karen Roach –
Christmas Present | Dreamstime.com

Zentangle® is a wonderful art form developed by Rick
Roberts and Maria Thomas. To learn more, to go
www.Zentangle.com

MY GIFT TO YOU

I appreciate your interest in my work, so I have a special gift for you. If you send an email to *HHHBonus@JoannaSlan.com*, we'll automatically send you a pdf with instructions for all of the Twelve Days of Christmas Projects—plus a handful of yummy recipes. In addition, we'll add you to my mailing list at no charge so you can keep up with future offerings, such as free books and free short stories.

All best from your friend,

Joanna

CHAPTER 1

People think that being pregnant is all about your growing belly, but the truth is, it also messes with your head. For every inch my waistband expands, I lose ten points of my IQ. Maybe it's because I don't get much sleep anymore. My skin itches, the baby pokes me with his feet, and indigestion causes a burning in my throat. Don't even get me started on the hormones. Whatever the scientific reason for my brain fog, I'm just not as sharp as usual.

My fiancé Detective Chad Detweiler and I were lying in bed talking one night before Christmas, when he said, "I've been thinking about baby names."

"Oh, you have?"

"Yes, in fact, I've been giving it a lot of thought. I think we ought to name our son Helmut Detweiler."

Thank goodness it was dark. I could feel my mouth flop open. I couldn't believe what he was saying. "Name our son what?"

"Helmut Englebert Detweiler. That's a good, strong German name."

I couldn't even respond; I was that stunned.

Detweiler continued, "We could call him Mutt for short."

I gasped.

"Mutt Detweiler. It has a certain ring to it," he said.

The bed started shaking.

Detweiler was laughing.

"You!" I pummeled him with my fists. "You had me going."

"Yeah," he said, chuckling. "You believed me!"

I sighed. "Wow. For a minute there, I was really worried."

Detweiler rolled over and raised himself on his elbows so he could stare down at me. "You shouldn't have been. You know I can't name our kid without your approval."

"And you guessed I wouldn't be in favor of Mutt?"

"I guessed."

I raised my head to meet his lips and kissed him. "Well, you guessed right."

CHAPTER 2

November...
Felton Community Center, St. Louis suburb

I love teaching Zentangle® because anyone can use its simple techniques to produce stunning pieces of art. Most of my classes are smallish, but that's fine because I enjoy wandering among my students and watching them work. While I usually teach Zentangle at my scrapbook and crafts store, Time in a Bottle, once in a while I agree to teach a class at an alternate location. When Ester Field Robinson invited me to share Zentangle with the Crafty Cuties, she offered to pay for my gas if I'd come to the Felton Community Center for the first three sessions.

"We've been having our meetings here for years. I know it's out of the way for you, but trying to teach old dogs new tricks won't be easy. Of course, we can't have all six of the classes there. They are booked solid in the run-up to the holidays, you see. But if we could start the lessons there, I can almost guarantee you that all our members will attend."

My friend and co-worker Clancy Whitehead

has complained that the word "no" is not a part of my vocabulary. She has a point. Before I realized what I was doing, I'd agreed to drive to Felton to teach six people. Definitely not a money maker.

Okay, so it wasn't the smartest business move I'd ever made. The upside was that I love Zentangle, and the classes are part of a series. The downside was that I had to haul my materials out to the car, in and out of the community center, into the car, and back to the store. Given my growing girth, all those moves would be tiring.

But seeing these women go from "I can't do that" to "wow, I did that!" would be well worth the effort. In fact, the class was as much for me as it was for them, because I could use a lot of stress release.

So it happened that the Wednesday before Thanksgiving, I found myself standing in a room in Felton, eagerly prepared to teach one of my favorite subjects. Over time, every teacher develops a patter, a way of talking about her subject and making the students feel comfortable. I always begin our Zentangle journey by administering a faux test to see if my new students have the skill necessary to learn Zentangle. First, I instruct them each to test their pens on a piece of scrap paper. Next, I ask my students to draw a line and a curve. When they are done, I ask them to hold up their work so I can inspect it.

Of course, everyone can draw a line and a curve! That's easy! Needless to say, I've never had a student flunk the test.

Once I've walked around and looked over their

scribbles, I shake my head solemnly and announce, "What a talented group we have! You won't have any trouble learning Zentangle. These two shapes form the foundation of every tangle. Now who's ready to learn?"

"That's all there is to it?" Eudora Field frowned at me. Eudora was Ester's sister, and the oldest Crafty Cutie. Actually, there wasn't anything remotely cute about her, but I tried to keep an open mind.

"Yes. The tangles are all combinations of curves and lines. Now let's get started."

Silly as it sounds, that little aptitude test sets aside their worries so my pupils can get down to the serious business of having fun.

My ruse certainly worked on the Crafty Cuties. After the test, six eager faces waited for further instructions. Okay, *five* eager faces. Eudora was frowning, but I felt confident I'd win her over.

"Are you sure you know what you're doing?" she asked.

That sounded confrontational, but I kept a smile on my face and tried to be reassuring. "I'm certified to teach Zentangle, and I've taught more classes than I can count. Zentangle can help you with your concentration, lower your stress level, and reduce any pain you might be feeling. There are studies ongoing, but we already know that it's a therapeutic marvel. Ready to do your first tangle?"

There followed a resounding cheer.

I held up a wipe board and drew Printemps, which is probably my favorite tangle of all time. "*Printemps* is French for spring," I explained.

"Every tangle has a name. The creator gets to christen his or her creation. Many of them are puns. Others have special meanings for the creators."

"Why?' asked Eudora. "Isn't anybody in charge?"

"The creators Maria Thomas and Rick Roberts are very inclusive," I said.

Eudora responded by muttering under her breath.

After my students got the hang of Printemps, which looks a lot like a pin curl, I showed them Crescent Moon, calling the half circles "ladybugs," a trick that never seems to fail to bring a smile.

As I tried to explain the variations, Eudora started talking to Caitlyn, the youngest of the Crafty Cuties. At eighteen, she's already a very talented young artist. Her grandmother, Ester, told me that Caitlyn hopes to attend a university with a great art program. Her dream is to support herself with her own creations.

Despite the fact I was ready to move on, Eudora kept her gums flapping. Caitlyn had to ask me to repeat instructions several times when we tackled Echoism, a take-off on a cursive capital L. For some it's a challenge, so I walked around and encouraged my students.

Last but not least, I showed them Hollibaugh, named for the husband of Molly Hollibaugh, an architect. "Molly is the daughter of Maria Thomas," I said, "and who are Maria Thomas and Rick Roberts?"

"The co-founders of Zentangle," said Caitlyn,

cheerfully.

"Who cares?" Eudora shrugged. "This is just doodling. What a waste of time."

"Except that doodling is aimless. It's hard to repeat what you do. Zentangle is deliberate, the patterns are like a vocabulary, and you can repeat what you learn. Caitlyn? Thanks for paying attention," I said. "This is for you."

I tossed her a small bag of Peanut M&Ms, a little treat I share to encourage participation.

Soon all my students were busily working on their tiles, the 3 ½ by 3 ½ – inch paper squares perfectly suited for Zentangle. All of them except for Eudora, who kept trying to talk loudly to her friends. Each time I moved to the wipe board to illustrate a confusing point, she'd raise her voice in competition.

In particular, she talked up a storm as I showed them how use their pencils to shade their drawings.

"Do I have to shade it your way?" asked Eudora with a petulant frown.

"Of course not," I said. "How you shade your work is entirely up to you. I'm only making suggestions."

With that, I began another slow tour of their tiles, stopping to praise each student. When I finished making my rounds, I said, "If you would, please, pick up your tiles. Sign the back and put them on the card table with the red plastic cloth. I want a photo of all the tiles. Take a minute or two to appreciate each other's work. Notice how you've all drawn the same patterns, but each tile is unique. Believe me, each of you will develop your own tangle style as you continue with this art form. It's almost as recognizable as handwriting."

"What's over there?" asked Eudora, pointing a gnarled finger toward the big display table.

"I brought in my portfolio of Zentangle designs, as well as several ZIAs, or Zentangle Inspired Art projects. Maybe you'll see something you'd like to try in a future class," I said. "I do have a favor to ask. Please keep your drinks away from our work. It's way too easy for a spill to happen. Don't even get near the table with any liquids, okay? Someone might bump into you, and then it would be all over but the shouting. Thanks so much for a great session, ladies. That's it for today. I'll see all of you here again next week."

With that, I erased the wipe board and started packing up my things. My throat felt as though I'd gargled with sandpaper. I badly needed a cup of hot tea. For most of the lesson, Eudora's bad manners had left no choice but to talk at the top of my lungs.

"Is Eudora always like this?" I whispered to Lois Singer, while the students began packing up. Lois has more enthusiasm than talent, but she is a nice lady. Her face bore the deep-set wrinkles that accompanied a hard life, but her soft brown eyes were kind, nonetheless.

"Unfortunately, Eudora has to always be the center of attention. We'd kick her out if we could, but out of kindness to Ester, we put up with her. They're sisters, you know. Eudora has five years on Ester. Here, why don't you take another muffin? Want a few for later?"

"Sure, but what I'd really like is the recipe," I

said, as I bit into my second homemade gingerbread muffin. One taste of its sour cream icing, I thought I'd died and gone to heaven. Talking around the food, I said, "I've had people talk while I present, but I've never had anyone who talked non-stop. It was almost as though we were in competition."

"You were," Lois responded with a tight grin. "Eudora competes with everyone. We count ourselves as lucky that she never had grandkids, because she'd insist on lording them over the rest of us. That's probably why she never married. No man could ever live up to her standards. She's a real piece of work."

"Nasty baggage." Cecily Kelly, another of the Crafty Cuties, joined us. Although Cecily has lived here in the US for more than two decades, she still talks with an English accent. "Eudora can't stand to see other people in the limelight. If I were you, I'd run right over and grab up my portfolio. She has an ugly habit of ruining other people's projects."

I paused while chewing the fragrant muffin and appreciating the zesty tang of allspice. "Ruining other people's projects? You mean while they're crafting?"

"Sometimes," Cecily said sadly. "Other times, she waits until they're done."

"Really?" I licked a little sour cream icing off my fingers. Standing on my tiptoes, I tried to see what was happening at the display table, but Esther blocked my view as she continued to gather her supplies.

"I'm sure since you're our guest, you'll be

fine. On the other hand, with Eudora you never—" Her warning was interrupted with a loud splash.

"Oh, dear!" Eudora turned her scooter toward us and showed off an empty cup.

I ran to the table where my work was swimming in a pool of Diet Cherry Coke.

Eudora shrugged. "Oops. My bad."

While I grabbed tissues from my purse and tilted the portfolio so the liquid would run off, she sat there, planted firmly in the middle of the mess, forcing me to move around her as I tried to contain the damage. When a pair of hands passed me paper towels, Eudora grabbed most of them almost as fast as I did. In a tug of war, she won. Calmly, as though my artwork wasn't taking swimming lessons, she dabbed at a drop of cola on her scooter.

"Here!" Caitlyn leaned over the far end of the table, pushing more paper towels my way. Ducking underneath, the young girl crab-walked to where the liquid was running down. She handed me a half a roll of toilet paper to mop up the mess.

Despite the fact she was impeding our progress, Eudora never offered to help. Nor did she move out of our way.

I was so angry I thought that the top of my head would fly off.

By the time I'd rescued my work, two beautiful pieces had been ruined.

CHAPTER 3

Later that same day...
Time in a Bottle, a scrapbooking and craft store in St. Louis

Ester called me at the store and apologized repeatedly. "My sister has had a lot of disappointments in life. She's a very bitter person. Sadly, she's decided to take her unhappiness out on other people. I can't tell you how awful I feel about your work, Kiki."

I counted to ten. The urge to say, "You can't feel half as bad as I do," was right there, begging to be shared, but I managed to hold back.

"I would like to try and make it up to you," said Ester. "I am calling with an invitation. Caitlyn is up for the Demski Award. It's being given Monday night at seven. As a nominee, she was given three invitations to share. Her mother was called into work at the last minute, and we hate to let her ticket go to waste. There's a fancy meal preceding it at the St. Louis Art Museum. I know this is late notice, but won't you come and be our guest?"

I love eating at the Art Museum, not only is the

food superb, but the ambience is fantastic. My calendar told me I had a free evening before our Christmas rush. I'd worked like a crazy person from October through Thanksgiving, getting ready for the holiday sales and for my maternity leave. Why not go and enjoy myself? Detweiler had been urging me to get out and have fun. Especially with the new baby coming.

"I would be honored," I said.

"I do have to warn you that my sister will be there, too. She's Caitlyn's godmother, after all. However, we can do our best to keep her as far away from you as possible."

Should I be petty and refuse the invitation? If I did, then Eudora would have succeeded in ruining more than my artwork. "No worries. Now, what's the dress code?"

CHAPTER 4

Monday, November 27...
St. Louis Art Museum

"Good luck, Caitlyn!" I held up my right hand to show my crossed fingers while Ester nervously grabbed my left.

All eyes turned to the front of the room, as the representative from the art museum smoothed his silk tie and stepped to the podium. Around us swirled a crowd of well-dressed and well-fed art patrons. The dinner had been outstanding, from the roast beef carving station to the table full of yummy desserts, including my current favorite key lime pie. I'd eaten so much that my elastic waistband threatened to snap.

Behind me, a deep voice said, "Ma'am? Please stay clear of the displays." I turned to see a security guard talking to someone hidden by the crowd. I tried to see who was being warned, but I'm short, so the other people blocked my view. Instead, I turned my attention to the front of the room as the man from the St. Louis Art Museum tapped the microphone.

"Is this thing on? Good. Now the moment

we've all been waiting for. I'm pleased to announce the winner of this year's Demski Award, which includes a four-year scholarship to Indiana University in Bloomington, Indiana," he said.

As he waited for the volunteer to hand him an envelope, he smoothed his tie yet again. While the transaction took place, I glanced over at Caitlyn. The girl was biting her lower lip in anticipation, and I couldn't blame her. This scholarship meant the world to her. Her parents were hourly wage earners who didn't have the sort of money that would allow her to attend such a prestigious school. An education from a place like IU would give her a leg up on making a living as an artist. The nearby Brown County Art Colony is one of six major art colonies founded in our country at the turn of the century. Even today, it's a thriving hub for artists of all kinds. Caitlyn would feel right at home there.

The young woman had definitely inherited her grandmother's love of crafting. Thanks to Ester's mentorship, Caitlyn had grown up trying her hand at all sorts of media.

Eventually, she'd settled on sculpting.

Caitlyn's entry for the Demski Award stood behind me on a three-foot tall plinth. She had sculpted a girl walking beside a lion. The human figure looked stunningly natural as she rested one hand on the majestic animal's mane. How Caitlyn had pulled off such a remarkable piece was beyond all my imaginings. According to Ester, her granddaughter had spent day after day at the St. Louis Zoo watching the lions, studying them, and sketching them as they moved around their enclosure. Caitlyn's "Girl with a Lion" fairly vibrated with life. She had managed to capture both the power of the king of beasts, and the innocence of the young woman.

It was hard to tear my eyes away from Caitlyn's statue, but I did. Someone in the crowd bumped my elbow, bringing my attention back to the presentation at hand. The small meeting room was packed with people, all waiting to hear who had won the scholarship. The work of a dozen students was represented, but Caitlyn's was the only three-dimensional piece of art. That alone made it a winner in my book.

The presenter stabbed his finger under the flap of the envelope. No one made a sound. I looked around but couldn't locate Eudora. As people instinctively stepped closer to the front, so they could hear the winner, I finally spotted her sitting in her scooter all alone, not far from the plinth.

The man at the podium finally pulled out a heavy cream card and scanned the name. Clearing his throat, he said, "I'm pleased to announce that this year's Demski Art Scholarship goes to—"

I squeezed Ester's hand.

"Caitlyn Robinson!"

"Oh! Oh! Oh!" Caitlyn threw her hand over her mouth. Tears sprang from her eyes as she turned to Ester. "Bubbie, can you believe it? Thank you, thank you for encouraging me. I could have never done this without you!"

The two women, one old and one young, grabbed each other in a happy embrace.

Over the hubbub of the crowd, I heard the

revving of a motor.

What a stupid time to run the vacuum cleaner.

"Congratulations, Caitlyn," said another young artist, coming up from behind to give Caitlyn a hug.

The motor revved again. This time louder.

"Way to go!" said a spotty-faced boy, as he clapped Caitlyn on the back.

She blushed a deep crimson. "Thanks, Eitan."

"Stop!" warned a voice behind us.

I didn't bother to turn around. All my energy was focused on Caitlyn as she graciously accepted one congratulations after another. The other entrants seemed happy for the girl.

"Can you believe it?" Ester wiped her eyes with a shaking hand. "My grandbaby's work will be here in the art museum for everyone to see and enjoy. Best of all, she'll be able to go to Indiana U. She's been wanting to attend that school ever since I took her to Brown County to see the artist community."

"It's unbelievable," I agreed. "I can't wait to put up a display about it in the store—"

But my sentence was interrupted by a loud crash, and a woman's scream.

The crowd parted. Ester and I turned toward the noise.

On the floor, in a million pieces, was Caitlyn's statue.

Right next to the mess sat Eudora. She had both hands on the steering wheel of her scooter, and she wore a great big grin on her face.

CHAPTER 5

November 28...
At Time in a Bottle

"What does the art museum plan to do?" asked Clancy. "They'll still give Caitlyn the scholarship, won't they?"

I stirred my peppermint tea. Boy, do I ever miss my morning jolt of real coffee. Lately I've been dreaming about tall frothy mugs of java. It's possibly the worst part about being pregnant, next to my growing belly and the hormones and the itchy skin.

"The art museum isn't sure what they're going to do. Primrose Levin heads the Demski Award Committee. She's known for being a stickler for the rules. I overheard her saying to one of the art museum mucky-mucks that the award money was in exchange for a piece of art, and if the art didn't exist..."

"Then the money couldn't be given out," Clancy finished for me.

"Exactly."

Clancy shook her head. "I can be pretty rigid, too, but that seems like an irrational response.

Why not let the girl make another piece of art?"

"Prim argued that point, too, saying it wouldn't be the exact same piece that won, so technically, it wouldn't qualify."

"Hmm," said Clancy. "But wasn't it the responsibility of the art museum to protect Caitlyn's work? This wouldn't have happened if they'd put the piece behind glass or secured the plinth more carefully."

I nodded in agreement. "To some extent, that's right. I heard the guard warn someone to stay away from the display. I'm willing to bet he was telling Eudora to steer clear of the statue."

The back door opened and Margit, my partner and co-worker, came in from the cold. Slowly she unwound her scarf and removed her cats' eye glasses that had steamed up from the changing temperatures. With deliberate movements, she took off her coat and hung it on a hook. "*Ach.* You are talking about that mess at the art museum, *ja*? It is not surprising, is it? I remember what that hateful woman did to your Zentangles?"

Actually, she misused the word "Zentangles." It's not a noun, but a proper name for an art form, but I didn't bother to correct her. We all knew what she meant.

Margit owns a percentage of Time in a Bottle. Not enough to have a large say legally, but I still value her opinions. I once tried to buy her out, but she got teary-eyed, so I never tried again. Since her husband is dead and her mother is in a care facility, this store is her reason for getting up in the morning. I didn't realize that at first. I do now. She's welcome to retain her percentage for as long as she wants.

"That's true," I said. "Eudora has a hateful streak. I don't think this was an accident. There's something more going on, some sort of senile dementia."

Margit poured herself a cup of coffee. Glancing over, she noticed my wistful look. "Soon," she said, "you will be able to indulge again."

"Not while I'm breast-feeding," I said.

"How about if I make you a cup of decaf?" asked Margit. She has a tendency to spoil me now that I'm as big as a Volkswagen. I admit that I love it. It's not like my own mother does anything kind for me. In fact, last week she told me, "You're as big as a house. Honestly, you've ballooned up like a whale in a National Geographic program. Have you no control over what goes into your mouth? That man is going to dump you. You'll be fat, pregnant, and unwed again!"

Charming, eh? Fortunately, my sister Catherine heard my mother going at me. Leaning over the back of Mom's chair, she whispered in her ear. Mom turned white.

"What did you say?" I'd asked Catherine later.

"I reminded her that you're pretty good with a gun, and then I pointed out that you haven't been your cheerful self lately."

She was right about that. I'd been in the dumps. Certainly, I missed my coffee. "I guess decaf'll have to do, Margit. Thank you. You know what? Even if Eudora has senile dementia, that doesn't change the outcome. She ruined Caitlyn's chances for pursuing her dreams—and she didn't even seem to care! The whole time everyone was trying to pick up the pieces, she sat there with a smug look on her face. It was shocking. Especially since she's Caitlyn's great aunt."

"If that was my kid or grandkid, I'd kill Eudora," said Clancy. "They'd find that old woman with scooter tracks all over her face. I wouldn't even dirty my hands doing it."

CHAPTER 6

Same day...

"Aren't you being a tad ambitious?" Clancy stared down at the e-blast I was sending our customers.

Staring down at the large monitor, I read the offerings once again. "Looks good to me."

But Clancy wasn't mollified. "That's a lot to take on, isn't it?"

She's in charge of scheduling all our special events and making sure we have the necessary supplies. Usually she sends out the e-blasts to announce what's happening. As the official "Queen" of these classes and demonstrations, she tends to get a bit huffy when I intrude, and she really kicks up a lot of dust when the calendar gets crowded. Not because she minds the workload. Clancy is a real trooper, cheerfully putting in the hours; in part because she has no other life. Since the divorce, her ex-husband has orchestrated an expensive campaign to woo their adult children over to his side. They've managed to forget that he dumped Clancy for a woman twenty years his junior. This store is everything to her. She puts on a pout when I get overly ambitious, because she's protective of our brand. Quality control is a big deal to her—and I appreciate her concern.

"Possibly," I admitted, glancing up at the calendar and noting that there was less than a month until Christmas.

"Totally," said Laurel Wilkins, our part-time employee and full-time friend. Laurel is always upbeat, so to hear her say that she was worried about my Twelve Days of Christmas class schedule surprised me.

I frowned at my friends. "Why?"

"Because you're eight months pregnant, that's why!" said Laurel. "Shouldn't you take it easy?"

"Bingo," said Clancy, throwing her hands up in the air. "My sentiments exactly."

"I don't have to teach all twelve classes," I said. "We already have crops scheduled. What's the dif? We need to have ideas, and classes, and crops, and to keep the momentum rolling right up until Christmas."

"Okay," said Clancy. "Let's go overboard, shall we? Then you can go into labor early, before you tell us what you have planned. That'll leave us to struggle through these classes looking like a pair of twin Dodo birds."

"Did you hear on NPR that a scientist is taking old DNA from preserved passenger pigeons and combining it with DNA from other birds to re-create the pigeons? Then they plan to move on to other extinct birds like Dodos and—"

Clancy used her hands to make a stop sign. "Wait a minute. You aren't dodging this that easily. How on earth do you expect us to teach all these different classes if you aren't here? We can't fill in if we don't know what we're supposed to do."

"We have Brawny, Margit, Laurel, you, and Rebekkah," I said. "That's five people not counting me. If each of you can learn two classes worth of material, then we're pretty well covered in case I go into labor. Surely you can manage to teach two classes each."

"*Ja*," said Margit, coming out of the back room to join us on the sales floor. Laurel straggled along behind her. "Kiki is right. We can't afford to slow down now. This is when we'll make most of our profit. I can learn two classes worth of material. So can each of you!"

Her enthusiasm put them to shame. I could see that Laurel, in particular, was having second thoughts.

"Look," I said, "these don't have to be really hard projects. The point is to think outside the usual stuff we offer. To boldly go where no crafters have gone before."

Clancy pursed her lips and glowered at me. "I think somebody has been spending too much time on Pinterest. We need to cut off your Internet access for a few days."

I laughed.

"She's probably right," said Laurel, "but I see where you're coming from, Kiki. Okay, I'm game. Come on, Clancy. We can do this!"

I gave Clancy a tiny punch in the arm. "See? You're the only hold out, girlfriend. We can give you all the really, really easy stuff because—"

"Because I'm all thumbs when it comes to crafting?" she asked indignantly. "Thanks a lot. Glad to know you've got such confidence in me."

"That's not what I said." I shook my head. "But if you're worried about learning new stuff..."

"I might be new at this, but I'm catching on fast. In fact, I'm pretty proud of my skills. Tell you what. How about if each of us comes up with two craft projects? Then we won't have to learn every class from Kiki? That'll leave us with only two of her sessions that might need covering."

Margit and Laurel nodded their approval.

I smiled. "Sounds like a plan. Okay, kids, the classes will start on December 12; that's two weeks away."

"Fourteen days from now!" groaned Clancy.

"Yes," said Laurel, "but our customers expect us to come up with something special for the holidays, so they won't be too surprised by our announcement."

"We can repeat the classes," said Margit, "if people want us to."

I nodded. "By Friday, December 1, I want to hear what you'll teach. I'll send out the finished e-blast announcing twelve days of classes. I will need your topics by then, even if you don't have all the particulars nailed down. Will that work?"

With the big task divided into manageable parts, I sat down to create a schedule and a form for me to use in announcing each of the classes. Meanwhile, the store came alive with activity and discussion, and I tried to hide the big grin on my face.

After all, I had reason to be pleased with

myself. I'd succeeded in turning my colleagues into Santa's busy elves.

CHAPTER 7

Friday, December 1…

Another Zentangle class had come and gone. Caitlyn, Ester, and Eudora didn't show up. The other Crafty Cuties were enthusiastic, but we all danced around the elephant in the room. The ruling on the Demski Award was still undecided. I could imagine that the Field-Robinson clan members weren't feeling particularly social.

Back at the store, things were humming.

"I have to admit that I'm impressed," I said, as I looked over the worksheets for the projects my crew had suggested. Even though they'd only had four days to come up with their ideas, they'd really outdone themselves. Now they would get busy working up samples to display in the store. "What I like most is the variety. We have classes here for all sorts of tastes and all levels of crafters. Well done!"

Clancy looked like the cat who'd eaten the canary. She was that proud of herself. "Plus, we each managed to turn our ideas in on time. You can write up a second email blast about the Twelve Days of Christmas Crafting Spectacular, and I'll send it out later."

"A few of our regulars already signed up," said Laurel, waving a sheet of paper at me. "They trusted us to come up with super ideas, and they didn't want to get left out if we ran out of space."

"Right," I said. "I offered Early Birds a 10% discount on the class price in the last newsletter. You probably forgot."

Margit reached down into a bag and pulled up a stocking cut out of scrapbook paper. "*Ja*, and I have finished the wish list stockings."

When she turned the shape around, we could see that she left a lined space on the back, perfect for compiling a "wish list." The top of the stockings had a small length of ribbon attached. This would allow us to use tiny clothes pins and hang the stockings from a sparkling cord running around the circumference of the store. When a husband or partner or friend wanted to know what to buy for one of our customers, we could point at the appropriate stocking.

"Don't forget," I warned my co-workers. "You need to use a red or green marker to strike through items as they are purchased. Otherwise our crafters might get the same article twice."

Laurel reached for the stocking that Margit dangled in the air. "These are seriously too cute. I love how you used white felt for the fur trim around the top."

Margit beamed with pleasure. The stockings were adorable. I knew she'd spent hours on them. We didn't have a die cut big enough, so she'd transferred the pattern and then laboriously cut out each stocking. Adding the fake fur trim and the ribbon involved yet another step. But she'd gotten her work done without complaining and on time.

"I finished these," said Rebekkah Goldfader, daughter of the late Dodie Goldfader, founder of the store. She held up beautiful blue dreidels. These would also be hung on a glittery string, but the dreidels would line the perimeter of the needle arts room.

"Love them," said Laurel, who had adopted the role of as our resident cheerleader. "The blues and purples are fabulous, Bekkah. Did you get the big menorah made?"

"Uh-huh," she said. From a bag at her feet, she withdrew a huge menorah made from discarded toilet paper and paper towel tubes. The flames were layers of red, orange, and yellow tissue paper.

"Terrific," I said.

"Kiki, do you still have more classes to teach the Crafty Cuties?" asked Laurel.

"It's on the schedule for Kiki to drive to Felton. The goal was to squeeze six classes in before Christmas," said Clancy, thumping a fingernail at a piece of paper. "What's up, Laurel?"

Laurel shrugged. "It piqued my curiosity. I read the article about the broken statue and felt so sorry for the poor girl who would have won that scholarship. What will she do now? Sounded to me as if it was broken on purpose. I can't imagine anyone who would be so mean."

I patted her arm. "You don't have to imagine it. You can come with me next Wednesday and meet this ogre for yourself."

CHAPTER 8

Back in October, Laurel was stabbed at an off-site crop. Since then she has been (understandably) skittish about any event taking place outside of the store. When I had suggested that she come with me to the community center, she had hesitated. Her eyes had widened, and her hands had balled up into fists.

"Okay," she had choked out.

"Great." I had tried to sound casual, as if I didn't know how much the agreement cost her.

The weekend came and went. A new week started. I wondered if Laurel had conveniently forgotten that she'd volunteered to accompany me to Felton. On Wednesday, she came to work as usual. She was bopping around the store that afternoon when I reminded her I was loading up for the Zentangle class.

It seemed to take Laurel forever to grab her coat, scarf, and gloves. Her lips were moving the whole time, so I suspect she was giving herself a pep talk.

"How are those EMDR sessions you've been going to for Post Traumatic Stress Disorder working?" I asked, as we climbed into my car. Her long legs made getting comfortable difficult, so she cranked back the seat.

"Really well. I'm much, much better," she said.

"Explain to me what EMDR means and how it works." This was both a chance for me to learn something and a way to distract Laurel by getting her to talk. But the words did not come easily. Out of the corner of my eye, I saw her start to talk, stop, and start again several times.

"Okay," she said, as she tapped her finger on her knee. As usual, she looked as if she'd stepped out of the pages of a Victoria's Secret catalog, in her sleek dark jeans, tight fitting sweater, and boots. Over the years, I'd come to think of her as a good friend. Given a chance, friendship overrides our senses, and we forget to examine each other closely. Instead of meeting face to face, we meet soul to soul. Once in a while, I would realize that I had quit noticing Laurel, the way you grow accustomed to a flower in your yard or a colorful tree in the fall. When I stop to appreciate her, to really enjoy her presence, her physical beauty never ceases to astonish me. Best of all, she is as lovely inside as out. Although you want to hate her for being so jaw-dropping beautiful, you can't. She's too nice!

Ever since the stabbing, she's been working hard to get over her fears, to overcome her nervousness about events outside of the store. "I don't want to be a captive here," she'd told me. The fact that she was next to me in the car spoke to the progress she'd made.

"EMDR is short for Eye Movement

Desensitization and Reprocessing," she said. "It's an eight-step protocol that helps a person revisit distressing memories and reduce their impact by using bilateral sensory input."

"Could you dumb that down? Way down? Stoop to kindergarten level?"

She laughed. "Okay, let me start over. Francine Shapiro, a young psychologist, was out walking her dog and thinking about a distressing incident. As she walked, she realized that moving her eyes from side to side reduced her angst. After exploring the phenomena systematically, she developed a protocol. Today, EMDR is used to treat a variety of psychological problems, including PTSD."

"How does it work?"

"You go through these eight steps and talk about the trauma while the therapist guides you. There are a variety of ways you do the bilateral movement. Some therapists have you tap your knees with your finger, left, right, left, right. Others have you follow blinking lights with your eyes."

"How does it work on your brain?"

"Oh," she said. "As I understand it, trauma swamps the brain and disturbs the way that you usually process upsetting events. The bilateral movement, along with the talking through the event, gives the patient a method of compartmentalizing what happened."

I turned south, noting as I did how the composition of the neighborhoods had changed dramatically. The southern portion of metro St. Louis always seems more muscular, more blue collar to me. So does the far north. By contrast, the area where Sheila lives and where Anya goes to school is decidedly hoity-toity, with an "I don't want to get my hands dirty" type of attitude.

"That's interesting," I told Laurel. "I can see why trauma would swamp your brain. Too much to process, and all those emotions coming on at once. What sort of problems can EMDR treat?"

"Phobias, panic attacks, post-traumatic stress are among the common ones."

"But does EMDR really work?"

"It did for me. Right after the stabbing, I didn't want to leave the house. When I drove within six blocks of the Lemp House, I got weepy and nervous. Even kitchen knives upset me. Honestly, I was at my wit's end until I heard about EMDR. There aren't a lot of trained therapists, but luckily, there is one in Clayton. She was excellent."

I mulled this over. "You might want to mention this to Eudora if you get the chance. Bring it up in conversation somehow."

"Eudora?" Laurel's expression turned pensive. "Have I met her?"

"I doubt it," I said.

"Back to your comment. Why should I mention EMDR to her?"

"Before I taught that first class to the Crafty Cuties, she made it a point to call and warn me that she's got a phobia about spiders. So much so, that she looked up the different tangles in advance and gave me a list of the ones that scared her."

"EMDR could definitely help with that. They also use it for addiction, eating disorders, and some have claimed it useful in treating people with borderline personality disorder."

"Huh," I said, as we pulled into the parking lot of the community center. "As if I could ever get my mother to see a therapist."

"Why not?" Laurel frowned.

"Because according to my mother, the only problem in her life is that we, her daughters, aren't doing exactly what she wants."

"And what does she want?"

"She wants us to worship her as a goddess. To cater to her every whim. To build our lives around her and accept her word as gospel." The words flowed out in a bitter torrent.

"I guess I poked the sleeping bear with a pointed stick."

"Yup," I said, "in the eye."

CHAPTER 9

With each passing month of pregnancy, it became harder and harder for me to carry boxes. My arms weren't long enough to reach around both my belly and a container. Consequently, I couldn't get a good grip on anything of any size. So I really appreciated Laurel's help in carrying my Zentangle supplies into the meeting room at the Felton Community Center. Most of the items were in small bags that fit into a fold-up cart, but a few of the deluxe Zentangle kits wouldn't fit.

She was making one last trip to my car when I heard her speak to someone in the hall.

"Oh! Brad! Uh, nice to see you. You work here?" The tone of her voice was uncertain. *Was this off-site event overwhelming her? Or was there another reason she sounded stressed?*

"I work here part-time," said a man's voice. "I've been applying to various police departments. In fact, I'm glad we bumped into each other. I've been leaving messages for you. Do you suppose you could clear up that thing?"

"Sorry about the telephone tag. I've been busy. What thing?" A distinct emotional overtone colored Laurel's voice. I dithered. There was a lot for me to unpack, but what if she needed me? *Should I go out into the hall and see what was happening? Or let it go?*

I slowed down so I could eavesdrop more efficiently.

"That thing where you lied and said I was stalking you."

Whoa! I juggled one of the packages of Micron pens, nearly dropping them.

"Brad, you definitely *were* stalking me. You left messages on my car, you showed up at my house, and you text-messaged me repeatedly. You even showed up at all my classes. And now you've started calling me again."

"I see it differently. You led me on. You're a tease, and you know it."

"No," said Laurel, keeping her voice neutral. "I am nothing of the sort. I was polite to you just like I am to anyone else I meet at school. The only times we interacted were in our study group. I didn't give you my phone number, and I don't know how you got it. I certainly never encouraged you to call me. In fact, I specifically asked you not to call. I never saw you outside that group, and I never encouraged you."

"That's baloney and you know it! You flirted with me. You wanted a relationship."

"I'm sorry if you got that impression, but that's not true."

Even from inside the room, I could feel the tension building out in the hall. I put down the pens and started for the door. Brad's tone was uncompromising,   while   Laurel   sounded conciliatory. I decided not to wait until things got more heated between them. Putting in an appearance might nip this problem in the bud. Besides, she could always tell me to buzz off if she wanted me to leave them alone.

I walked to the door and hesitated. The way it stood half-open, I could linger there and not be seen.

"You just keep telling yourself that, okay? Deny it all you want," Brad said, "but that letter in my file is keeping me from getting hired. That's not fair!"

"I see," said Laurel.

I hesitated. All I needed was to take one step forward, and Brad would realize that Laurel was not alone.

"Do you? Are you getting the picture? You need to get that letter taken care of—and it needs to be done fast. I mean it, Laurel. This is bull—"

"Hello," I said in my perkiest voice, as I made my grand entrance. "I'm Kiki Lowenstein. I don't believe we've met."

"Brad Oxemann," he said, extending his hand.

His handshake was actually a mean-spirited squeeze that hurt. I did my best not to wince. I hate it when men bully women like that.

"Hey," he said, sizing me up, "you're that woman who hangs around with Chad Detweiler, right?"

"That's one way of putting it. Detective Detweiler is my fiancé," I said, emphasizing the word "detective." For good measure I added, "Robbie Holmes is my father-in-law."

Brad's face darkened. He'd caught my drift,

and he didn't like the implication. Not at all. "I'm in charge of security here," he said, jerking a thumb at his chest. "I hope you're not parked in one of the reserved spaces or I'll have to have you towed."

Inwardly, I responded with, *Is that the best you can do, sonny boy? If so, bring it on!* But outwardly, I stayed cool, calm, and collected. "No, I'm not in a reserved space. But I do need to interrupt your visit with Laurel because I need her help."

"Yeah, right," said Brad, narrowing his eyes at me. The way he swept his vision up and down my body made me uncomfortable. "Pregnant and ready to pop. Oh-kay. I get it. Right. Laurel, I've got to get back to work. Think about what I told you. That letter really is not cool."

Before he walked away, he did that stupid hand gesture where you point your index and first fingers at your eyes and then at the other person to say, "I've got my eyes on you."

Instinctively, I moved closer to Laurel, in a show of solidarity. She said nothing, but I felt her shiver. Slipping my hand behind her back, I found her fingers and gave them a squeeze. Together, we faced Bad Boy Brad down, but that gave me scant comfort. I wasn't sure we'd seen the last of him.

"What a creep," I said, when he'd disappeared from view.

"You don't know the half of it."

CHAPTER 10

Laurel and I went back into the meeting room and unpackaged the rest of my supplies. Once we had everything unloaded, we surveyed the layout and decided we needed to arrange the tables in a horseshoe shape. As we tugged and shoved, Laurel fumed about Brad.

"He's such a jerk. The professor assigned us to the same study group, and all Brad did was ogle me. When I told him I was seeing someone else, he refused to believe it. Joe even dropped by to pick me up after the study group so that Brad could see I was telling the truth. That didn't work. Nothing did. He followed me around all the time. It was totally creepy."

"Wow," I said. "Sounds pretty intense."

"Even the other students noticed. A couple of them went to the prof and complained about how Brad was acting. I probably could have ignored him, but he really went too far when he started tagging after me in his car. I had an appointment with my ob/gyn and actually bumped into Brad in the waiting room. He'd told the receptionist that he was my boyfriend, and he was worried about me. I think that woman was two seconds away from telling him everything he wanted to know. The worst part is that he can be totally charming. Totally convincing. I think he's a psychopath."

"Ugh." I shuddered at the thought, but I wasn't surprised. One psychologist has estimated the number of psychopaths in the prison population as at least twenty percent. The number in the general population has been estimated at anywhere from 4% to 20%. To my untrained ear, this guy Brad sounded like he fit the description perfectly. "You need to be very, very careful, Laurel. That's a sick young man."

"I know. He always struck me as seriously creepy. He can blame my letter all he wants, but I suspect there are a million other reasons why no police force wants him."

I set out the watercolor paints we would be using for this session. "Please tell me that you don't plan to remove that letter."

She lifted a long strand of blond hair out of her eyes. A troubled expression clouded her beautiful face. "That would be irresponsible of me. What if he does the same thing to someone else? I have Joe to watch over me, and my Uncle Johnny. Another woman might not be so lucky."

"I agree." Changing the subject, I said, "Let's see. We've got the individual sheets of paper from the watercolor pad. The empty tuna cans for water. Plastic storage containers of sea salt coming right up."

"What will they do with the salt?"

"Sprinkle it on the paper after they paint it. The salt lifts up the moisture, making cool splotches. You remember? You've done this with me before."

"Uh-huh," Laurel said, but she sounded unsure. The pout on her pretty face told me that her mind was miles away. Brad had gotten to her, destroying her hard-won equilibrium the way a tornado moves through a trailer park.

Usually I'm a fan of second chances, but Brad Oxemann had to be stopped. If she withdrew the letter, and if he was accepted into the law enforcement community, he would have free rein to menace women. Given the power of a badge, his abusive nature could get entirely out of hand.

"You're absolutely right. Asking to have that letter removed would give him carte blanche. He squeezed my hand really hard when we met."

"He always does that!"

"I'm only sorry that you ran into him here. In fact, he must be new, because I've never seen him here before."

Her sweet smile was tinged with sadness. "I'm usually a very lucky person, but today my rabbit's foot isn't doing its job."

"You carry a rabbit's foot? That's so not like you!" I couldn't help but laugh. Laurel is a vegan who doesn't even like to wear leather.

She reached into her purse and pulled out a rabbit's paw. On closer inspection, I realized it was made of fake fur. At my expression of surprise, she laughed out loud. "I wanted a lucky charm and my old roommate Chelsea thought I needed one, so she concocted this. There's even a crystal in it and herbs and rolled up scrolls of prayers. Pretty funky, huh?"

"I think it would make a great Christmas gift for the discerning animal lover. Someone like Anya. A real rabbit's foot would send her into orbit!"

"Hmm." Laurel took it back from me. "Fake rabbit foot charms. I'll have to think on that."

CHAPTER 11

Caitlyn Robinson was the first Crafty Cutie to arrive. Her feet were dragging, and her eyes were downcast as she entered the room. The girl was walking through sadness so thick, it stuck to the bottom of her feet.

"Oh, Caitlyn," I said, throwing my arms around her. "I'm glad to see you! You poor kid. Any word on what the Demski Award committee plans to do?"

"Sorry we missed class last week." She pulled back from my hug to shake her head. "No decision yet. They're meeting at the art museum next week. I guess that a representative of the Demski family plans to attend and hear the pros and cons. It's not looking too good."

"Honey, I am so sorry. You must be devastated."

"Pretty much. I put so much work into that piece. You know how some pieces really live up to your vision and some don't? That one did. It was magical. I doubt I can replicate it, even if I try. I mean, of course, I'd give it a shot, but…" a trembling finger wiped away a tear, "it's looking kind of hopeless."

"Caitlyn, this is my friend and co-worker, Laurel Wilkins," I said.

Laurel and Caitlyn exchanged polite greetings.

"Kiki showed me a photo she took of your piece," said Laurel. "I was blown away by how beautiful it is. Was. I'm so sorry that it was broken."

"My grandmother is taking it really hard. She keeps saying she should have kept an eye on Great Aunt Eudora, so it's her fault. I've told her it isn't. We all know that she is a pain in the butt. She's got a screw loose. No one expected her to do anything so destructive, but it is what it is, right?"

"Did Eudora say she was sorry?"

"Nope." The girl gave a little laugh. "According to her, she couldn't hear, being in the back when the crowd moved forward. Eudora says the finger accelerator somehow got stuck. She says it's not her fault."

"But I heard the guard warn someone to move away from the plinth. That had to be her. Surely she could have chosen a different path!"

"Right," said Caitlyn in that sarcastic voice all young people have mastered brilliantly. "Eudora says that the scooter had been acting crazy for a long time. She blames my dad for not fixing it. But Dad's a great mechanic. He couldn't find anything wrong! Not before the award ceremony, and not later when we got back to Eudora's house."

I wondered if she'd always called her great aunt by the woman's first name, or if this represented a further widening of the breach between them.

Caitlyn sniffled, found a tissue in the pocket of her jeans skirt, and blew her nose. "I don't know who to believe or what to think. My mom has always hated Eudora. She puts up with her because she's family, but Mom says we should have expected this to happen."

That confused me. "Come again?"

"Grandma says her sister has always had a mean streak. She doesn't like it when other people are happy. Eudora says that life is all about learning to live with sorrow. Mom thinks that's one of the reasons they didn't invite her to become a nun."

"Wait a minute!" Laurel's eyebrows flew up. "You're talking about Eudora Field? Wasn't she supposed to become a postulant at the Monastery of Visitation?"

"Right," said Caitlyn. "That's her. She started out at Viz as a teacher, and later she did tutoring on her own, privately. Latin and Spanish. She did substitute teaching at some of the public schools and ran some of the Spanish clubs."

Laurel's face brightened in recognition. "I had Miss Field as a teacher. She taught my Latin class at Viz."

"Boy, oh, boy," said Caitlyn, shaking her head. "I bet that was a crummy experience. She has the patience of a mosquito."

"That's true," said Laurel with a terse laugh, "and she absolutely despised me from Day One, and let me know it. Until I recognized the name, I'd blocked the whole experience out."

"Whoa. Go back to the part about her hating you. What do you mean? Everybody loves you, Laurel!"

"That's sweet of you, but it's also a big fat whopper. Miss Field took one look at me and decided we were not going to get along. End of discussion. You see, I developed early. Even though we wore uniforms, she always thought I was dressed inappropriately. My clothes were either too tight or falling off. My mother didn't have much money after Dad walked out, so she made me wear my clothes as long as possible before we went shopping for new things. Then Ma would buy stuff one size too big, so I'd have room to grow, but those things were enormous. What a mess that was!"

Hard for me to conjure up a picture of Laurel in poorly fitting duds. However, a very real tinge of pain colored in her explanation. Her melancholy tone convinced me she was dead serious.

"Mom says that being turned down for the nun-hood, or whatever you call it, really did Great Aunt Eudora in. But that was years ago. Lately, she's just gotten worse and worse. Her doctor thinks she might be having little strokes. He says she's lost her filter. Like she ever had one," said Caitlyn.

"Maybe that's what happened. Maybe she had another one of those strokes and—"

But I didn't get to finish because Caitlyn interrupted with, "No." Looking down at her nails and aggressively picking off bits of metallic blue polish.

"I think she was actually planning to ruin my work—and she did. Mom doesn't know it, but earlier that day Eudora and I got into a fight. She said I would never win the Demski Award, because I'm not talented enough. Life is one long series of disappointments, she told me. According to her, I should prepare myself for things not going my way, and then she reminded me that I'm nothing special. I told her she was a mean, bitter old woman, and that all of us wished that she'd died a long, long time ago."

CHAPTER 12

With that Caitlyn excused herself to go wash the tears off her face.

Laurel, meanwhile, put on a brave expression and got right down to business. "Where would you like the food? You sure picked cute napkins to go with the Christmas cookies."

Oh, boy, I thought. *So much for the holiday spirit. This is going to be heaps and heaps of fun.*

I sincerely hoped that Caitlyn could keep from crying during the class. I prayed that neither she nor her grandmother would allow their quarrel with Eudora to tarnish our time together.

"That table off to the side will do." I pointed and Laurel dutifully trotted over to set up the goodies. What were the odds that Laurel, the girl who got along with everybody, would accompany me to an off-site session and bump into not one but two people she'd rubbed the wrong way? First Brad and now Eudora Field?

Jeepers.

Caitlyn came back and offered to help Laurel. I excused myself to use the restroom, something that happens frequently because my unborn son insists on using my bladder as a trampoline. After washing my hands, twice, I stared into the mirror and lectured my reflection. "Chin up. Brad the Bad has gone about his business, and maybe Eudora won't recognize Laurel. Even if she does, what's the big deal? Eudora is already on everyone's poop-scoop list, thanks to her stunt at the Demski Award. You, Kiki Lowenstein, are a professional. You are here to teach a class, and you will do exactly that, no matter what sort of mood your students are in."

That made me feel slightly better.

CHAPTER 13

Rather than walk directly back into the classroom, I wandered down the hall to the big glass doors. One look outside at the weather, and I started thinking that Caitlyn might be my only student. Light snow had been predicted, but whether we'd get a White Christmas was anyone's guess. Right now, the rain was coming down like angry pinpricks, splatting against the glass. The ice crystals struck hard, slowly melting and trickling down.

As I stared out into the parking lot, I saw Eudora's Prius with the handicapped hang tag. I knew I should go out and help her, but I couldn't bring myself to open the door. Then I saw Brad walking toward the vehicle. In short order, she was motoring up the handicapped ramp. When she got stuck, he helped her by giving the vehicle a tiny shove. In the process, he also managed to knock loose one of the panniers, the leather pockets strapped to the back.

Her notebook, papers, and other items tumbled out onto the wet pavement. Brad motioned for her to go on, and he picked up her belongings. His kindness almost encouraged me to change my mind about him.

Almost.

While he was bent down, Cecilia Kelly and Ruby LeCuero scuttled by. They must have noticed what was happening, because they'd taken care to walk on the far side of the parked cars. That way, neither Eudora nor Brad saw them.

Their little detour told me volumes about their relationship with Eudora. Both Cecilia and Ruby are lovely people. Under most circumstances, they would have surely stopped to help, but as I watched, they hurried toward the doors without a backwards glance.

I intended to walk away from the door before they saw me, but I didn't hustle fast enough. That left the three of us to stare at each other guiltily.

"We're bad," admitted Cecilia.

"Please don't tattle on us," said Ruby. "It's just that Eudora is mean to everyone. We put up with her for Ester's sake, but we certainly don't like the woman."

"When she's around, things have a tendency to go pear-shaped," said Cecilia.

"Pear-shaped?" I repeated.

"That's Brit-speak for 'badly,'" explained Cecilia.

Ruby grinned. "It's like she speaks a foreign language, isn't it?"

Cecilia laughed. "You know what they say. The US and England are two nations separated by a common language."

That caused me to giggle as we headed back toward the classroom.

CHAPTER 14

Cecilia wasn't the only one who wanted to keep her distance from Eudora. When I walked back into the classroom, I discovered that the other crafters had come in the side door and seated themselves in a group. They'd purposely filled up one table, so that Eudora would have the other one all to herself.

This worried me. What if Eudora made a fuss? The whole point of Zentangle is to get into a meditative groove, one that promotes relaxation and allows you to let go of stress. I held my breath as Eudora came rolling into the room. But being ostracized did not seem to bother her at all. In fact, she appeared to be pretty pleased with the arrangement, probably because she had a tendency to spread her supplies and take up more than her fair share of space. Thanks to their shunning of her, Eudora was able to plop down right in the center of a table, throwing her jacket to her right and smiling approvingly to her left.

That's where her good mood ended, however. Everyone else started getting out their supplies, while Eudora just sat there and folded her hands.

She wore a smug smile on her face.

I wondered what she was thinking.

Perhaps her grandniece had been right. Maybe she was slipping a cog. She certainly did not appear eager to learn a new skill. During our first class, she wouldn't draw a line without asking me for help. Rather than try her hand at what I demonstrated, Eudora would sit and stare at her paper. I make it a habit to walk around and examine each student's work. As I got near to Eudora, she would toss down her pen so it would roll onto the floor.

Time after time, I would squat down and pick it up for her. To an outsider looking in, it must have seemed as though I was doing weird pregnancy aerobics. Down and up, up and down, in first position with my feet spread wide. Instead of a *port de bras*, I kept one hand on the table as I lowered myself. I have to admit it was a great workout for my thighs. After a time, my muscles started to spasm. With each retrieval, Eudora seemed more pleased with herself. She enjoyed seeing me struggle to chase down her pen.

"You can't expect me to do this! I don't know how!" she shrieked, as I offered one new tangle after another.

I felt like saying, "Of course you don't know how to do this! That's why we call it a class. You're here to learn. And you can't learn if you don't try! Babies throw down their pens."

Fortunately, I had managed to keep a civil tongue in my head. But the memory still bugged me. Especially today. Caitlyn and Ester sat side-by-side with their pens and notepads ready, while

Eudora folded her hands in a prayerful position. She had done nothing to get ready. In my head, I replayed the crash of Caitlyn's statue. That made me even angrier. All the other students seemed eager to listen and learn. But not Eudora.

A glint in her eyes seemed to challenge me.

To what purpose, I couldn't guess.

Time to move on.

"Hey, everybody," I said, by way of greeting. "Good to see all of you."

All of you? Okay, that was a lie. I could have done without Eudora.

"Most of you have probably met Laurel Wilkins, my beautiful and talented assistant, because you've seen her at my store."

"Happy holidays!" Laurel stepped up beside me and waved. In her long dark jeans and cobalt blue sweater, she looked like a fashion model. No one would ever guess that the loosely woven scarf around her neck covered a knife wound that had nearly taken her life.

"That's right," said Ruby. "Laurel helped me pick out the papers for my daughter's graduation invitations."

"An hourly wage job at a craft store," said Eudora. "I'm not surprised."

I felt my jaw drop. Laurel shrugged off the insult. Her smile never wavered.

I wasn't about to let that unkind remark go. "Actually, we're lucky that Laurel still finds time to help out at Time in a Bottle, because she is currently a doctoral candidate at Washington University."

Eudora made a loudly dismissive sniffing

sound while the other women beamed with approval.

"Okay, then, let's get started," I said, trying to sound cheerful, but my enthusiasm had waned significantly. "Today we're going to work on four new tangles. Then we're going to paint paper with watercolors. You'll take the painted paper home to use on a craft project that you'll bring back next week. If you would, please pull out your notebooks. I want to dive right into these new tangles because one of them is rather challenging."

All of the students except Eudora were ready to go, with their pens poised over their blank notebooks. They were hanging on my words, ready to copy the "step out" or the illustrated instructions that would help them replicate today's tangle.

But Eudora just sat there, stony faced as an Easter Island icon, glaring at me and at Laurel.

"Eudora? You might want to take this down," I suggested in as sweet of a voice as I could muster.

"We need our notebooks?"

"That might be helpful," I said, while mentally counting to ten rather than scream, "Yes! You ninny!"

We all waited while Eudora fished around for hers. She opened a flap on the pannier bags strapped on the right of her scooter. That didn't produce the desired notebook. Flashing me a crooked grin, she said, "Could have sworn it was in here."

Next she opened the pannier on the left. After digging around a bit, she took out the tablet and laid it flat on the table in front of her.

The other women had their notebooks open. Eudora's was closed.

I thought about waiting, but I'd had enough of her playing games. If she didn't want to follow along, that was fine by me.

"I am now going to draw W-2 for you," I said, turning toward the wipe board. "This particular pattern starts with a grid, so use your pencil and put down four—"

"Eeek!" Eudora screamed and grabbed her chest.

CHAPTER 15

Lois raced across the room and got to Eudora first. She somehow managed to grab the older woman before she toppled off of her scooter.

Ester hurried to her sister's side and began digging around in Eudora's panniers. "Where are they?" she asked, as she searched through the pockets. "Her nitro pills! They should be in here!"

I dialed nine-one-one and gave them our location.

Laurel grabbed a bottle of water and carried it over to Eudora's table. Ruby unscrewed the top and offered a sip to Eudora, but the woman only thrashed around.

Stepping out into the hall, I caught a glimpse of Brad Oxemann's retreating back. I shouted, "Help! Emergency!" but he didn't turn around.

I hot-footed it to the community center front desk. "Medical emergency," I shouted. "Does anyone here know first aid?"

One of the two women grabbed a white case with a red cross painted on the top and followed me back to the classroom. I could hear the other one repeating our address into the phone.

When I rounded the corner and raced back into the room, all I could see were the backs of the women. They were all bent over Eudora's prone form. Laurel was administering CPR. Lois spelled her after a few minutes. The two worked together seamlessly. The woman from the front desk handed me the Red Cross kit and ran off to flag down the ambulance that was on its way.

Ruby got to her feet.

She shook her head. "No heartbeat. No pulse. She quit breathing. Lois and Laurel know what they're doing, but still..."

All of Eudora's supplies—her pens, her pencil, her notebook, and the tiles—had clattered to the floor. Her pens and pencil had rolled in opposite directions.

They would be easy to trip over, so I snatched them up as I called nine-one-one again to tell them what was happening.

"Stay on the line with me please," said the dispatcher. "Is she still breathing?"

"Two people are giving her CPR," I said. "She's not breathing on her own."

I watched, feeling helpless. By the time the EMTs came racing into the meeting room, Lois and Laurel had taken turns puffing into Eudora's mouth and pressing on her chest for ten minutes. Lois seemed a little woozy from the effort as the medics helped her to her feet. Laurel continued the compressions until a tech told her to back off so he could take over.

We all took a giant step backwards to let the uniformed men do their work.

As one of them worked on Eudora, the other

asked Ester questions about her sister's general health and medical history. Ester's voice quaked, but she answered everything succinctly. "What I can't understand is where her nitro pills went," said Ester. "My sister always has them on her."

In short order, the EMTs had Eudora loaded on a stretcher. Ester ran along behind them, begging to get to ride with her sister. The sharp smell of rubbing alcohol permeated the air.

But another scent caused me to turn around. Being pregnant, I'm super susceptible to fragrances, and this was the smell of cheap cologne.

Brad was standing at the end of the hall, watching the medics and staring at us.

"You could have offered your help," I said. "I saw you. You must have heard me."

"Get lost, chubby," was his response.

I'm not usually a vengeful person, but I vowed then and there to tell Robbie what I'd seen. I'd make sure Brad's reputation preceded him when he next applied to become a law enforcement officer.

Because he headed up the county police, Robbie had a lot of friends among the 91 municipalities that make up what most people call "St. Louis." When word got out that Brad had stood around with his thumbs up his nose rather than helping, his already slender chances of finding a job in the law enforcement community would fade to nil.

I shook my head, thinking about Brad's nonchalance. When I walked back into the classroom, the space that had seemed so full now echoed with emptiness. One by one, the other women came over and stood beside me. We joined hands, staring at each other. We were shocked, exhausted, and totally rattled.

"At the risk of sounding calloused," said Cecily, but then her voice trailed off.

"We might as well let Kiki teach her class," said Marvela Castillo. Whereas Cecily has that famous peaches and cream complexion often associated with women from the UK, Marvela is a dark-haired and dark-eyed Cuban.

"There's nothing more we can do for Eudora. Ester is with her, and so is God." Ruby fingered her rosary as she spoke. She is a cancer survivor who attributes her remission to her faith.

Caitlyn stood off to herself, her arms wrapped around her waist, as if she was trying to hold everything together.

"Caitlyn? Are you all right?" I put a hand on the girl's arm.

She buried her face against my shoulder. "It's been a rough month."

"I know it has, sweetie," I said, patting her back. "Would you like for me to go ahead and teach the Zentangle class? It might relax all of us."

Although I'd put it out there, I was surprised by how fast Caitlyn reacted. "Would you, please? I'm so sick of my great aunt and the drama that follows her around. I mean, sure, I feel sorry for her, but geez. She keeps ruining one good thing after another."

"How about this?" I turned to the small knot of women. "We take five minutes to wash our hands and grab a drink. Then we'll proceed with the class, after Ruby leads us in a prayer for Eudora."

"Sounds like a plan," said Cecily.

The other women nodded in solemn agreement.

CHAPTER 16

Despite my best efforts to teach a good class, by the end of an hour, we were all too emotionally exhausted to go on.

"Zentangle has been proven to calm your nerves and soothe you," I explained. "I hope that when you get home, you'll whip out your supplies when you feel stressed."

"It's okay, Kiki," said Lois. "You don't have to sell us. I do feel better, but I can't shake that image of Eudora clutching at her chest."

"I can't either," said Ruby. "To think it happened so quickly, too. One minute she was dragging out her notebook, pleased as punch that the rest of us were waiting, and the next she's crumpled over and not breathing."

Marvela sighed. "Reminds me of that last episode of the Sopranos, you know? One minute we're looking at Tony and the next there's no sound, no picture, and no credits. I thought my TV was on the blink, but my husband said, 'Isn't that the way? We don't know what's next.' He got that right."

Caitlyn kept looking at her cell phone, hoping

for word from her grandmother. She sent a few text messages, but those didn't generate a response.

"Don't worry about it, hon," said Lois, patting the girl on the shoulder. "She's probably too busy to answer you."

"Or maybe they won't let her use her cell phone," said Marvela. "When my husband had triple bypass surgery, they told us cell phones weren't allowed in the family lounge."

Caitlyn nodded. "I guess. I'm trying to think positive, but I can't shake this bad feeling. It's like the summer when the sky is clear, but the maple leaves roll belly up and you know there's a storm coming."

I needed to get us off the sad topic, so I said, "Caitlyn, can we put your aunt's scooter in your car? I hate to leave it here, and I don't have room in my little convertible for it."

"Whatever," she said, reminding all of us instantly that she might look grown up, but she was still a teenager.

Laurel and I bundled up and followed Caitlyn to her Hyundai. Working together, the three of us lifted the scooter into the trunk.

"Drat," I said, as Laurel and I walked back into the empty classroom. "Blame it on my pregnancy brain. We should have sent Eudora's things home with Caitlyn."

"No biggie. Their next class is back at the store, right?"

"Right. All the rooms in the community center were booked up until Christmas, so I offered to let them take the rest of their classes at Time in a

Bottle. I figure the more warm bodies through the front door, the better the chance of making a profit this season."

Laurel smiled at me. "Sure, sure. The truth is that you're the original Mrs. Nice Guy, and even though the store will be a mad house, you'll manage somehow, won't you?"

"Yup."

Fortunately, I always bring along over-sized zippered plastic storage bags when I pack for an off-site class. Today they came in really handy as we scooped all of Eudora's things into one. Her notebook had fallen to the floor during the excitement. Once again, she'd managed to make me do an awkward squat for her. Because the notebook had landed under the table, I practically twisted into a fat pretzel shape as my fingers swept the indoor-outdoor carpet, trying to get a purchase on the spiral bound papers. When I finally nabbed it, I dragged it to me and plopped it into the bag without looking at her work.

Frankly, I'd had enough of Eudora for one day.

Maybe even for a lifetime.

CHAPTER 17

Laurel and I climbed into my old BMW. This was one of those nights when I desperately wished for heated seats. For the most part, with pregnancy came a soaring body temperature that made me impervious to the cold, but my backside still felt the shock of contact with frigid leather. Laurel shivered, too. However, the low temps were quickly forgotten when I told Laurel about Brad walking the opposite way when I was yelling for help.

"What a jerk!"

"The least he could have done was to come and see what the matter was!"

"Yes, and he could've stuck around and helped us load that heavy scooter into the car. But he's not like that. He's a real creep," said Laurel.

"That's readily apparent," I said, as I navigated the dark streets. "Maybe it's just as well that Brad didn't stay. He makes my skin crawl."

"You noticed that, too?" asked Laurel. "It's like there's this ugly aura. One of my other classmates petitioned the instructor to be moved to another study pod."

"Do you believe in evil?"

"I guess," said Laurel. "I want to think that there's good in all of us, and that environment plays a huge role in how we become who we are, but..."

I started to comment, but unfortunately my phone buzzed. While I dug around for it, I decided against saying more. I didn't want to share what I knew about her background. Laurel was a very private person, and she'd never mentioned to me that my old friend Mert Chambers was her biological mother. I wouldn't have known either, except Mert blurted it out in a moment of panic. In fact, I found myself wondering just how much Laurel actually knew about her conception.

Laurel is the product of a rape that occurred while Mert was a minor in foster care. Because Mert was so young, and without any legal rights, her foster parents had forced her to sign away her baby.

"Maybe it was for the best," Mert had told me over a bottle of wine. "I couldn't have raised her proper-like. Not in that environment. At least she got herself a chance. Mrs. Wilkins did right by my baby girl, even if her husband did run off and leave them high and dry."

There are so many questions I would love to ask Laurel. I wonder if she knows that her father was a rapist. If so, does that change the way she sees herself? Is Laurel so sweet because she is overcompensating for her father's genes? What happened to her biological dad? Has anyone kept track of him?

As I headed down the dark streets, I bit my lip rather than blurt these out. I was sincerely curious, but I'm sure they would be invasive.

A buzzing sound filled the car.

"I think that's your phone," said Laurel. When I finally found it—as usual, it had migrated to the bottom of my purse—I held it up so we both could read the message: *Great Aunt Eudora died of a heart attack—Caitlyn*

"Wow," I said.

"Funny, isn't it?" Laurel shook her head at me. "Last week after Eudora knocked over Caitlyn's entry for the Demski Award, everyone wanted to kill her. But now she's dead, and I still feel sad about her passing."

I pulled up to a stop sign and stared her straight in the eye. "You know what's really going on here? We aren't sad that Eudora is dead. We're relieved—and that's what makes us both feel so terrible. Can you imagine? To me, that would be the ultimate disgrace, to leave behind people who felt relief rather than sorrow at my passing. It would mean that I hadn't added value to this world. That I hadn't earned my keep as one of God's creatures. Isn't that the least we owe our Creator for all this splendor? To make a mark, to effect a change, to lighten a load, to do something to repay Him for this gift of life?"

"But what about when you get old and confused or sick?" wondered Laurel. "What then? Your passing might come as a relief."

"But that's a different sort of relief. That's the sigh that comes when you put down a heavy load. It's not the same as the sensation of being freed from the clutches of an unkind person."

Laurel nodded. "In one instance, your relief comes because this person you love is no longer suffering. But on the other hand, it's your personal suffering that's come to an end."

"Exactly."

CHAPTER 18

Pulling up to the garage of our new home in Webster Groves always put a smile on my face. Two huge coach lamps bracketed the garage door. Their golden light spilled down onto the glistening snow, warming a frozen landscape. Best of all, I could go right from my car into the house without stepping outside. To me, this was the height of luxury. For three years, I'd put up with parking my car in the elements, and in St. Louis, that means every sort of weather imaginable except for a sand storm. I've seen hail as big as baseballs in March, snow storms three feet deep in October, and tornadoes that turned the skies green and ripped the roofs off buildings in August.

Even so, I love living in "the Lou." There's so much to see and do!

In particular, I adore Webster Groves, aka the Queen of the Suburbs. When we first moved here, Anya and I rented the small cottage that Leighton Haversham (yes, *that* Leighton Haversham, the famous author) had converted from a detached garage into what he hoped would be his writing studio. As he worked on the project, Leighton went overboard, adding a kitchen and building out two bedrooms and a sitting room as well as a bathroom. There was even an alcove between the kitchen and bedrooms that could be used as a huge storage area or a small bedroom.

But the location didn't work for him as a writing studio. Leighton's one of those writers who can't handle any sort of distraction. Being in the middle of his garden proved too tempting for him. He would sit down at his word processor, realize his marigolds needed to be dead-headed, pop up, putter around in the flower beds, and get nothing done. After spending an entire year and producing not a single chapter, he gave up. Luckily for me, he decided to rent the cottage at the same time I was looking for a new home.

"My ideal writing spot is a place without any windows," he had said to me.

"You could have used that storage area off the kitchen," I'd said.

"I didn't even think of that! Besides, I needed help with Monroe and Petunia. You and Anya are godsends."

Petunia is Leighton's scaredy-cat pug, a little boy dog who acts more like a pansy than a petunia. Monroe is Leighton's rescue donkey. While Leighton was serving on the board of the St. Louis Zoological Park (that's the proper name for our world-renowned zoo), he learned about Monroe, a quadruped who'd taken a dislike to anything in diapers. The donkey had adopted the habit of head-butting anyone short and dressed in white from the waist down. That proved a huge problem because Monroe was supposed to be the star attraction in the Petting Zoo.

Instead, the board was forced to consider whether Monroe should be sold to a meat-packer for dog food.

"It had been *considered*," Leighton had told me, putting a special emphasis on that one word, "but not seriously discussed. We were looking at all options, but the minute I heard that Monny might get the death penalty, I knew I had to take action."

Somehow, and I don't know the exact mechanism—nor do I want to know—but somehow, Leighton managed to get Monroe's local citizenship approved by the Webster Groves City Council. That's how the donkey came to live on the grounds of Leighton's family home.

To my way of thinking, the tiny roughly hewn shed that shelters Monroe adds heaps and heaps to the charm of Leighton's yard.

"Those logs? They came from a log cabin that was falling apart on a piece of land over by St. Albans," he had explained to me. "There weren't enough left to rebuild the entire cabin, and I hated to see this piece of history crumble into sawdust."

An architect viewed the tumble-down cabin, drew up plans, and used what was left of the old structure to make a charming "new" shed with storage for gardening implements and a riding lawn mower. Leighton had been picky enough to demand that the "new" shed be built the old way.

"You've seen the log cabin at Grant's Farm? Grant's original shelter, the place he named Hardscrabble? He notched his logs just the way we did these. Of course, many were already notched on one end, but I had the builder notch the other end so they matched." Leighton was justifiably proud of the workmanship.

"How did you chink it?" I asked. "Chinking" is the act of filling in between the logs.

"First of all, you have to realize that the logs are only stacked against each other, with a space between to allow for expansion and contraction. Then think about the settlers and what their world was like. They could only use whatever was on hand. So some cabins are chinked with corn cobs, small sticks, and moss between the logs."

"What about mortar?" I wondered. "All the photos I've seen show a grayish-white mortar between the logs."

"That's the daubing. It's a three-layer process. First you have the logs, then the chinking, and the daubing is the sealant layer."

I thought about all this as I pushed the button to close our garage door. The wind howled and a stray leaf blew in, seeing a safe place to hide until spring. The intricacies of log cabin construction had served to make me more grateful than ever to have a snug roof over my head. The "big" house had been built by Leighton's ancestors nearly a hundred years ago on the banks of the Mississippi, and moved to this location by Leighton's grandfather. This sturdy brick structure is of the Federal/Greek Revival style, a classic in every sense of the word.

Yes, this is a grand old place. One that I'm privileged to call home.

CHAPTER 19

"Mama Kiki! I saw it! They's flakes! From the sky! And I catched them, but they melted!"

A short figure in SpongeBob Squarepants pajamas raced through the kitchen and hurdled himself at me. I dropped my purse and squatted to hug Erik, my five-year-old son.

"You saw the snow? Wow! That's so exciting!" I said, planting a kiss in the crook of his sweet little neck.

"I did! I did! Anya sawed it too! Is it still falling from the sky? Will it come again?" The words tumbled out of him.

"When I came in, I saw a few flakes. One or two. I'm pretty sure we'll get more as it gets closer to Christmas." I stayed low so he could look me in the eye. He's adjusting to his new life pretty well, although he still has bad dreams once in a while. The fact that he's gone from never calling me by name to calling me "Mama Kiki" has been a huge step.

No matter how tired I am after a long day at work, Erik's raw enthusiasm never fails to lift my energy level. With the advent of Christmas, he has a lot to be excited about. For one thing, Erik has never seen snow. Born and raised in California, he came to us when his mother, Detweiler's first wife, Gina, died in an auto accident with her husband, Van Lauber. Although Erik was not Detweiler's biological child, Gina had legally been married to him at the time of Erik's birth and listed him as the father. She gave Van's sister, Lorraine (aka "Aunt Lori"), a letter for Detweiler, admitting her infidelity to him, while begging him to raise her child.

Although Aunt Lori would have loved to raise Erik, she has a progressive form of MS that is incurable and that makes it impossible to keep up with an active little boy. Furthermore, her prognosis is grim. It's highly unlikely that she'll live to see Erik enter high school.

Detweiler had flown out to California and brought Erik back to live with us. He also brought along Erik's nanny, Bronwyn Macavity. Brawny, as we call her, is a Celtic warrior through and through. She'd lay down her life for any of us.

While reflecting on all the boy's losses, I hugged him tightly. Erik is a precious, precocious child with huge brown eyes, skin the color of a latte, and reddish hair that curls around his adorable face. He's very curious about his new baby brother. A bit skeptical really. Who can blame him? The fact that my body is an incubator for an infant is a miracle that even I find hard to come to believe.

"Is the baby going to see the snow?" Erik asked, putting a hand on my belly.

"I hope so," I said. "Probably. The baby will

come after Christmas. We usually get an ice storm."

"What's an ice storm?" Erik wrinkled his nose.

"That's when we get a mix of snow and rain. It freezes on all the tree branches—"

"And the world looks like a fairyland!" said Anya, joining us.

I stood up to hug my thirteen-year-old daughter, who is already taller than I am. Considering all the changes in our lives, she's doing a terrific job of keeping her balance. Growing up as an only child, she's never had to share her home or her mother. Fortunately, Anya's sense of compassion outweighs her natural selfishness. Sure, Erik bugs her from time to time. All younger siblings do. But she's really handled herself remarkably well, all things considered. I believe that her generosity of spirit is one reason why. Because Anya lost her father two years ago, she knows what it's like to lose a parent. She extends to Erik the sort of kindness that can only come from having endured a similar loss.

"How was your day, sweetie?" I said, reaching up to smooth a stray lock of Anya's platinum blond hair.

"Okay," she said. "I'll be glad when the holidays are over. The teachers are trying to pack everything in at the last minute before we go on break."

"Not cool," I said, shaking my head. "Erik? How was school today with Miss Maggie?"

Maggie Earhart is an old friend of mine. Her daughter is in the same grade as Anya. The fact that she wound up being Erik's kindergarten teacher is a real bonus. Knowing his background, she's showered him with extra attention and affection.

"Jeffrey Pearson bit Bella Roscoe," said Erik, solemnly.

"You have to be kidding me!" I shrugged off my jacket. "That's awful! What did Miss Maggie do?"

"She gave him a carrot and told him that carrots are for biting, not people," said Erik.

"That's right. Carrots are for biting," I said, trying to keep a straight face. "What did Jeffrey Pearson say?"

Erik spread his arms wide in a gesture of total defeat. "Jeffrey says he still likes people best."

CHAPTER 20

Detweiler didn't get home until after midnight.

"Brr, your feet are like icicles," I said, as he climbed into our bed.

"Lucky for me that you're as hot as a coal-fired furnace." He threw an arm over me and pulled me close so we were spoons.

"I guess, but when I was coming home tonight, this furnace didn't put out enough heat in my tushie. I couldn't help but long for heated seats in my car! What a luxury!"

He nuzzled my neck. The feel of his beard against my skin awakened other longings. I rolled over and kissed him.

"We need to talk about getting you another car," he said, coming up for air.

"What a boring conversation."

"Maybe," he chuckled, "but one we need to have. That old BMW has been a lifesaver, and I know you kept it because it didn't have any Blue Book value, but we might need to trade it for a small SUV."

Scarlet, my private name for my red car was one of the last ties to my first marriage. Although

I didn't harbor a lot of good thoughts about my life with George Lowenstein, that candy-apple red car was a bright spot. I hated to think about letting it go. Sure, St. Louis isn't exactly known for its balmy weather, but on those days that the temperature is right, I love driving with the top down. To be honest, I also love the way the car handles. It has a turning radius smaller than a donut. And pick up? Let's just say that the car's torque has saved my life more than once.

Detweiler slipped a finger under my chin. "I can hear you thinking, thinking, thinking. I know you don't want to give up that car, but it might be time to move on. The cost of insuring it and another vehicle will be too much for our budget."

I nodded, fighting the lump in my throat.

"Let's talk about something else," he said, pulling me closer, so I could rest my ear against his chest. "How was your day?"

Needless to say, my recitation left him speechless.

"You still awake?" I asked, talking directly to his pec muscles.

"Yes," he answered. "Brad Oxemann. What a total loser."

"So you remember him?"

Detweiler's laugh was soft and ironic. "Unfortunately, yes. You know how it is when you get sick on food? The taste lingers in your mouth? Brad's like that. What a miserable excuse for a human being. He thinks I stopped him from advancement, but I didn't. Every single one of his instructors flagged him as unsuitable for a career in law enforcement. He's immature, trigger-happy, rigid, hot-tempered, cruel, and he has no respect for authority."

"Those are his good points, right?" I gave Detweiler a tiny punch in the arm.

"You've got it. Although I guess he's good at Spanish. Even considered majoring in it in college."

I told him about Laurel reporting Brad as a stalker.

"Wouldn't surprise me one bit. You need to warn her that he's dangerous," said Detweiler. "He likes to brag about how many guns he owns."

"Geez." I shivered. "Can this get any worse?"

Detweiler kissed the tip of my nose. "It already has. Brad dropped by the Felton Police Station. He claims that Eudora Field was murdered, and he's named Laurel as a suspect."

CHAPTER 21

"What?" I jerked my head back so I could look Detweiler in the eyes. Even though it was mostly dark in our room, the moonlight did provide a touch of illumination. I thought my fiancé might be joking.

"You heard me," said Detweiler. "Fortunately, the desk sergeant is an old friend of mine, Constantino Greanias. He placated Brad, sent him packing, and then called me."

"When were you planning to tell me all this?"

"Tomorrow morning. I figured it could keep overnight."

I rolled away and pushed myself into a seated position. From there, I stood and wobbled my way to the bathroom. When I came out, I said, "If you think I can sleep after that, you've got another think coming."

He threw off the covers. Since he sleeps in drawstring flannel pants and a white tee shirt, he was dressed for padding around the house. "How about if I make you a cup of chamomile tea?"

Ever since my friend Cara Mia Delgatto moved to Florida and made a new pal who swears by chamomile, we've been drinking more of it. Detweiler knows it's a natural soothing brew. He was right to suggest it, even though I wish he could have poured me a glass of wine instead.

Gracie, my Great Dane rescue pup, had heard us tiptoe through the house. She must have pushed open the door of Anya's room to join us. Leaning hard against Detweiler's knee, she stared up at me with loving canine eyes while the tea kettle came to a boil.

"How on earth does he figure that Laurel hurt Eudora? I was standing not twelve feet away, explaining how to draw a tangle, when she clutched her chest and slumped in the seat of her scooter. Since Eudora came in last through the door, and because no one wanted to sit with her, she took a seat on the far side of the tables. Laurel couldn't have even gotten to Eudora without walking in front of me!"

Detweiler turned off the stove. "He didn't have any evidence, although he was full of accusations. There was something about Eudora Field having had Laurel as a student years ago, and how that didn't end well."

He measured out the chamomile tea into the clever brewer he'd found for me at Teavana.

"Eudora was Laurel's Latin teacher at Viz. According to Laurel, she had complaints about the fit of her uniform. Go figure. Like that doesn't happen in every high school in the country when you've got a buxom young girl who develops early."

"So Laurel didn't tell you that Eudora was a proctor for the SAT? And that she accused Laurel of cheating?"

He let this sink in as he took his customary spot, leaning against a kitchen cabinet, standing three feet from our kitchen table. His long legs were crossed at the ankles and his arms folded over his chest.

Boy, did he ever look sexy. I finished my tea.

"No, she didn't mention the accusation." My mouth felt dry as cotton. Detweiler saw me trying to swallow and poured a glass of cold water.

"Even so," he said, handing me the drink, "I can't imagine Laurel killing the old bat."

The water and his conclusion both made me feel better. "Neither can I. Although at least two other people in the room had their own reasons for wanting to see Eudora dead."

CHAPTER 22

The next morning, we sent out an e-mail blast announcing Eudora Field's passing and suggesting that our crafters sign the card we posted by the cash register. I planned to go to the funeral, but it was listed as "family only," so instead we sent flowers. It seemed like the least we could do, considering I'd been standing nearby when she keeled over.

The following days were crazy busy. Both my children attend CALA, the Charles and Anne Lindbergh Academy. The school always has a lot of politically correct "seasonal celebrations." This year was no exception. Our weekends were packed, too. Detweiler's parents invited us to the family farm for a sleigh ride and dinner. Then we helped the older Detweilers cut ivy and evergreen boughs to decorate our homes. Then came Monday and more work at the store. For each class we do, there's an enormous amount of prep. Most of our free time was eaten up with "kitting." When you "kit up" a class, you divide the materials so that each student has exactly what she needs and not much more. For example, if the project calls for a button, instead of handing over a container of buttons, you give each student one button. That means a dramatic cost savings in your supplies category.

It's the planning stage that makes or breaks our profit margin. First you have to determine what you need, then you source and order the components, and finally you allocate only as much as each student needs.

Over the years, I've learned that the best approach to kitting is to set up bins and assemble the packets as if we run a miniature factory.

"Let me get settled and I'll run off the handouts for your classes," said Clancy, as she entered the back room, stopping to shake tiny spitballs of snow. They rolled like tiny marbles down the front of her black cashmere coat. "On my way into work, I picked up more color cartridges for the copier."

"*Ach*," Margit muttered, "that is not good. The office supply stores charge too much. Better to order them online."

Clancy looked a little cross. "I usually order them online, but we ran through all our surplus ink because of Kiki's Twelve Days of Christmas promotion."

The two women glared at each other.

"Stop it, girls," I said, wagging a finger at them. "We knew this was a big task, and that it would throw us a lot of curve balls. We're all doing our best. Clancy, did you drop by The Muffin Man?"

The Muffin Man is a bakery formerly run by Cody, whose real name is Jonathon, but recently sold to his nieces, Emma and Jesse. Confusing, eh? All you really need to know is that their goodies are outstanding. Because the shop is on Clancy's way to the store, she's tasked with picking up our treats.

Okay, the *other* reason we send Clancy is that no one trusts me not to eat all our order!

"The cupcakes and cookies are out in my car," she said.

"I will go with you to get them," said Margit, rising from her seat at her desk.

"No, I'll help you bring them in," I said, getting up from one of the folding chairs surrounding our staff snack table.

"Oh, no, you won't," said Clancy. "It's slick out there."

"Oh, yes, I will," I said, pulling on the cape that Brawny had made for me. What a handsome piece of clothing it is! The outside is navy wool, with a stand up collar and gold buttons. The inside is lined with fake red fur. Leather straps buckle it over my expanding girth.

Ignoring Clancy's protests, I stalked out the back door.

She was right. What had started as light snow had changed into clumps of flakes and finally become sleet. My feet scrambled for a purchase on the asphalt parking lot. Clancy scuttled over and grabbed my arm.

"You never listen, do you?"

"We can't let Margit do this," I said, "If she falls, it could—"

I stopped. I didn't need to tell Clancy how devastating a fall could be for Margit. Her own mother, Mrs. Clancy (my friend goes by her maiden name because her real first name Druscilla is too horrible to use), recently took a tumble in her assisted living apartment. The fracture caused her to have a blood clot. As a result, Mrs. Clancy has slipped into a coma.

"Sorry," I said, giving my friend a quick hug.

Her eyes were moist. "Don't be. My mother was too vain to use a walker. She's paying for her pride."

I stopped and turned to Clancy. "All of us are deeply flawed. The imperfection runs through us like a vein of black carbon through a piece of marble. We just have to keep praying that we can work around it."

Clancy nodded. "But I forced her to move from her house into the assisted living after that first fall. Maybe if she would have stayed—"

"She would have broken her neck tumbling down those stairs."

Clancy looked away. "Yes, that was a real possibility."

"Or she could have fallen at home and died on the floor, all alone."

"You're right." Clancy linked arms with me. We made our way slowly to the car. "Have you decided what to do about your mother?"

"No, she's getting meaner and meaner every day. I can't believe some of the garbage that's coming out of her mouth. After the holidays my sisters and I need to sit down and talk. Amanda's been living next door to Mom for years, and she says that Mom is definitely getting more and more cross. All I know is that a constant drip, drip, drip, of negativity has to be emotionally devastating for my sisters."

"How's Catherine taking it?"

"She avoids Mom. Unfortunately, Amanda can't avoid Mom as much as Catherine does. Mom's accustomed to calling on Amanda for errands and other sorts of help. Amanda told me that Mom's really wearing Catherine down. She starts the minute Catherine walks through the door. Complaining, whining, you name it."

"At what point is it enough?" asked Clancy, turning loose of me so she could unlock her car door. "When is it fair for us to say, 'You are killing me'? How much do we owe our mothers? My mother cared for me for eighteen years. I've been caring for her for twenty-five. I think it's safe to say that there were moments of joy in those first eighteen years, but in the twenty-five I've taken care of her, there's been nothing but misery. You remember how it was. She would fight me at every turn. Her demands kept escalating. She called me at all hours of the day and night to complain. But I still wouldn't have moved her out of her home and into assisted living if she hadn't fallen."

"I remember. I don't think my sisters and I can wait for Mom to fall. You made that move because of your mother's health. We might need to make a change because of my sisters' mental health. Shouldn't they count, too?" I asked, as I reached forward to grab the white cardboard box of cookies out of Clancy's hands.

The shift in my weight caused my feet to slide. I scissored back and forth like an ice skater.

"Kiki!" shrieked Clancy, putting down the box and reaching for me.

I threw my arms out to grab her. That shifted my center of balance even farther. My feet flew up and out from under me.

CHAPTER 23

The landing knocked me breathless. Maybe I was even unconscious for a second or two. All I can say for sure is that when I opened my eyes I saw nothing. The world had gone black.

"Kiki? Kiki!" Clancy screamed my name.

I turned my head toward the source of the noise.

Bright light haloed her face, obscuring her features.

Was this the famous light at the end of the tunnel?

Had Clancy turned into an angel?

"Am I dead?"

"Good grief, I hope not!" she said, as she reached for me.

I stared up at a universe of shapes in metal, plastic, and wire, all colored the same sooty gray with smudges of green and orange.

Clancy grabbed the edge of my cape and tugged at me.

But I was stuck, caught under her car.

"You're going to have to help me because you're hung up on something."

The undercarriage pinged and dinged as it cooled from being driven. When I lifted my hands to find something to push against, I could feel the heat.

"No can do. The car's still hot!"

"Dag nab it." Clancy was on her hands and knees looking at me.

Tires crunched on ice. She turned to see who had joined us.

"Laurel? Thank goodness you're here!" Clancy rocked back onto her haunches.

A pair of fashionable high-heeled boots came into view. They stood next to Clancy's knees.

"Clancy? What are you doing?" asked Laurel. "Did you drop something?"

"Kiki," Clancy said.

"You dropped Kiki?"

"No! She slipped. She's under there." A perfectly manicured finger pointed my way.

Laurel's face appeared in that thin sliver between the car frame and the ground. "Oh my! Kiki, what are you doing down there?"

"Checking her alignment."

"Okay," said Laurel, tentatively, "but shouldn't you get up? Aren't you cold?"

"She can't. She's caught on something," said Clancy. In my mind's eye, I could see her rolling her eyes as she delivered this bombshell.

"Not my fault!" I yelled. "The car's too hot for me to push against with bare skin."

Clancy rose to her feet. That left me staring at a pair of black booties next to the brown, high-heeled, fashion boots. The toes turned toward each other. It was like watching a bizarre shoe commercial on TV.

"We need to help her," said Laurel. "That'll take getting down on the ground. I have a blanket in the trunk of my car. Let me grab it. Do you have anything in yours?"

"Two pieces of carpet," said Clancy.

"Do they match?" I yelled.

"Of course they do!" she called down to me.

That figured. She was Miss Girl Scout, always prepared. Every Midwesterner knew that jamming a piece of carpet under spinning tires could give you traction. She probably also carried a twenty-pound bag of kitty litter and a bag of salt.

"Go ahead and get the carpet squares. We can kneel on them. I'll get down on one side, you get on the other, and you can tug at her while I push," said Laurel.

Clancy's trunk creaked open with a protest. Two burgundy pieces of carpet hit the pavement next to me.

Using the carpet squares to pad their knees, Laurel and Clancy got down to my level. Between them they shoved and tugged.

I didn't move an inch.

"Kiki? Have you got a pair of gloves?" Laurel asked. "Because if you do, you could put them on. Maybe then you can touch the underneath of the car and get some leverage."

Reaching in my pocket was awkward, but I managed. The stink of the oil was starting to make me sick to my stomach. My fingers found one knit glove. I managed to hold it with my teeth and wiggle it on. Even using my covered hand as leverage, I couldn't move. The heat of the car had melted the ice under me. Water was seeping into my clothes. I shivered. If the ground I was lying on had been frozen, I might have been able to slide out, but it wasn't.

"That's it," said Clancy, brushing her hands together. "I'm calling nine-one-one."

CHAPTER 24

The longer I was under the car, the colder I became. Initially, I hadn't felt the low temp because the car was still warm. As Brawny had predicted, the wool cape had kept me warm despite the moisture it had absorbed. However, the black denim maternity pants I was wearing were now soaked, and they transmitted every bit of the cold to my skin. By the time the firemen dislodged me, I was shivering so hard I thought my eyeballs would fall out of their sockets. Since I was so unsteady on my feet, one man on each side walked me back to the store. Laurel grabbed her blanket from her car and brought it to me. Stepping into our warm bathroom, I changed out of my wet clothes and wrapped the fuzzy pink fabric around my body.

"It was your buckle," said Clancy, holding up my wet cape. "That's what caught under my car."

"No wonder I couldn't scoot out."

Margit contributed a big safety pin to my outfit, and I carefully pinned my makeshift sari in place so it wouldn't fall down. But that style left my shoulders exposed, so Margit ran into the sales floor and returned with a beautiful blue shawl she'd knitted. With her help, I wrapped it securely around my shoulders. It smelled like her, a combination of mothballs and rose water.

"This shawl is the one that was hanging on the wall? I hate the fact you had to cannibalize a display just for me."

"*Ja,* and it is for a very good cause," said Margit. "I am making you hot chocolate. You are still cold. I can see that."

Turning to the five men who now crowded our back room, she added, "There is fresh coffee in the pot, and I can make each of you tea or hot chocolate, if you'd like."

"No, thanks," said the tallest of our guests.

"Please," I said. "It's the least we can do."

"We have cookies and muffins, too." Clancy opened up one of the pastry boxes.

That got the men's attention. Especially because the cookies were thickly frosted with a wonderful vanilla-scented icing.

"I can't believe how cold I still am," I said. My teeth were chattering so much that I had trouble getting the words out.

A pounding on the back door alerted us. Clancy opened up to a pair of EMTs. As she explained what happened, she started giggling. So did Laurel. Soon the entire back room was in hysterics—except for me.

"Her baby bump got her stuck under a car?" marveled a young EMT as he took my temperature. "That's a new one."

"Ha-ha-ha," I said, for the second time that day. "It was the buckle on my cape, not the size of my belly."

The EMT checked me for signs of a concussion; I shook with cold on the same folding chair I'd vacated earlier. The hot chocolate was working to raise my temp, but slowly.

"Does your head hurt?" he asked, as he shone his flashlight into my eyes.

"It's tender where I bumped it, but otherwise, no."

"Let's get a look at your baby bump."

The firefighters kindly bid us goodbye so I'd have some privacy.

Obediently, I tugged away the blanket to expose my bra and my abdomen. The medic prodded me with cold, but skillful fingers. He listened for a fetal heart beat and counted. Just then Baby Detweiler kicked to let me know that he didn't appreciate the activity happening right outside his temporary home.

"I landed on my backside. Honestly, I don't think my tummy was involved in the accident." Nothing was painful, and the EMT found no signs of bruising.

"I text-messaged Brawny. She's bringing you dry clothes," said Laurel.

"You seem to be okay," said the EMT. "Tonight you should have someone wake you up every hour. If you start feeling sick to your stomach, then you need to visit an emergency room. Also, watch for any signs of labor. You might want to follow up with your own doctor tomorrow. Tell us again how you wound up under the car?"

"I slipped."

"She slid under so fast that I didn't have a chance to grab her!" said Clancy. "One minute, I was turning the key in the door on the driver's side and the next she vanished."

"And you couldn't get out, why?" asked the second EMT.

"Because the buckles on my cape got snagged. The undercarriage was too hot for me to touch. I couldn't unhook myself, and I couldn't get any leverage. Look, I have one very, very important question that needs answering."

"What is that?" The EMT put his stethoscope and flashlight back into the first responder's bag he carried.

"Are there any of those reindeer-shaped cookies left?"

CHAPTER 25

Both of the EMTs left shortly thereafter, which was fine by me because I didn't want to share any more cookies.

"Kiki, I hate to upset you further, but we have a problem." Laurel couldn't meet my eyes.

"We do?"

"I do, and so I guess you do, too."

Clancy looked up from the computer where she'd been working on scheduling. Margit's ears perked up, too, although she wasn't as obvious with her interest.

"Spill it," I said. I'd finally warmed up, although I wasn't too crazy about my outfit.

"I got pulled over this morning on the way here."

"I have told you that you drive too fast," volunteered Margit.

Laurel's lower lip quivered. This was so not like her that I went over and put a hand on her back. "You okay?"

"I wasn't speeding," she said. "That's what has me worried. It was a Felton cop, but he stopped me as I was getting on 40."

My heart went into overdrive. "What did he say?"

"He made me get out of the car and leave the door open. Then he made me put my hands on the roof of my Avalon while he patted me down."

Flashes of that horrific scene from the movie *Crash* whirled through my head.

"Was he inappropriate?" I asked.

"No." Her hands were shaking as she pushed a piece of hair out of her eyes. "H-h-he said he'd gotten a call from another driver that I was driving erratically, but I wasn't! Honest!"

"Brad Oxemann," I said.

"I think he was behind this, yes," she agreed. "There's no other explanation."

"Who or what is a Brad Oxemann?" asked Clancy.

I explained about the security guard at the Felton Community Center.

"Can Detweiler help?" Margit adored Detweiler, and she thought he could perform miracles. Although Detweiler was nice to all my friends, he was particularly kind to Margit because she reminded him of his late grandmother. Coming from the same German stock, they had an instant bond. When Margit spoke German to my fiancé, he grinned like a little boy.

"I hope so," I said, giving Laurel a hug. "Or maybe Robbie can. I'll talk to him tonight. He and Sheila are coming to our house to light the Hanukkah candles. Is there a way to keep you off the streets? Can you have Joe come and pick you up after work?"

"No," she said, "he's doing a Hanukkah first night service at his church. But I'll see who else I can call. Maybe Johnny can come and rescue me. Maybe Margit can give me a ride."

"It's going to be okay," I told her.

Clancy raised an eyebrow at me. I knew that look. It was her way of saying, *Don't make promises you might not be able to keep.*

CHAPTER 26

Brawny arrived soon after with my dry change of clothes. Since I had her, Laurel, Margit, and Clancy all in one place, I decided we should have an impromptu staff meeting.

"Clancy? Could you try to get Rebekkah on Skype?" We'd recently learned how to use the service, and I'd found it invaluable for holding meetings. Now that there were six of us, it had become problematic to get us all in the same place at the same time. Thanks to Skype, we could use the computer to chat with everyone.

Being the logical, methodical thinker she is, Clancy quickly mastered Skype. I could do it with effort, but Clancy treated it like an auxiliary telephone with a camera. In a matter of minutes, she'd rung Rebekkah and patched her in.

"Before the store gets too busy, I thought we'd review our Twelve Days of Christmas Crafting Spectacular," I said. "Margit has offered to teach the first of the Twelve Days of Christmas sessions."

"I can't believe how cute these carol singers are," said Clancy, as she picked up one of the small musicians I'd devised using scrapbook paper and toilet paper rolls.

"They sure are. By the way," said Rebekkah, "be sure to tell your friend Cara Mia that our customers loved the paper bag dreidels. They were a real hit. That pre-Hanukkah class was our best attended session so far."

"I will. I actually owe Cara Mia a call. She said she might make it up here before Christmas, and I want to know what her plans are. I guess they're having a holiday party at the restaurant, and she plans to attend." I turned my attention to our oldest crew member, "Margit, are you feeling confident about teaching this class?"

"*Ja,*" she said. Her eyes were bright behind her cats' eye glasses. "I have been over the instruction sheet. It is very good. Very complete."

"The hardest part is transferring the patterns onto paper, but you already know how to do that, and so do most of our customers. After that, it's a matter of cutting and gluing down the parts."

She picked up one of the carolers. I'd created a set of three, two men and one woman. Each was dressed in Victorian fashion. The men wore paper top hats with colorful bands, while the woman balanced a big bonnet on her head. Their paper arms held black notebooks of music.

"Remember, folks can add as much bling as they'd like. In fact, I suggest you encourage sparkle."

"I know, I know!" Margit sounded impatient. "I can take care of this!"

"Tomorrow, I teach icosaohedrons twice. Once to our general population, and later to the Crafty

Cuties."

"Thursday I'm teaching the crocheted necklace," said Brawny. "Margit, have you got the gold crochet thread ready?"

Margit scowled at Brawny. "What? Do you think I'm a *dummkopf*?"

CHAPTER 27

This antipathy between Margit and Brawny needed to be dealt with, but it would have to wait. Originally, they had bonded over a love of needle arts. But as time went on, they discovered that they took a wildly divergent approach to their crafts. Margit followed patterns slavishly. Brawny worked instinctively. Both methods had their strong points. If the pattern was true, Margit's end product came out perfectly. If the pattern was flawed, and this happened frequently, Margit would be at a loss about how to make an adjustment. Brawny did this automatically, but because she didn't pay attention to patterns, you never knew what the end product would look like. Usually, the finished garment would be a close cousin to what she intended, but once in a while, the item would morph dramatically into something totally unexpected.

They had managed to keep their differences civil until the day that a customer brought up World War II. As a result, we nearly had World War III right then and there on the floor of Time in a Bottle.

"My baby brother was killed!" Margit had shrieked. "The bombing! The planes! We were children! Innocents!"

"You destroyed our cities. My grandmother was hit by falling bricks and died! You started the war, what with your racism and greed," Brawny had said, in a cold, flat tone that scared me more than Margit's wail.

"Ladies!" I had pushed them apart because they were in each other's faces. "That's the past. We live in the present. Get a hold of yourselves! Quit it or I'll throw cold water on you both."

They had backed off, but they had glared at each other like two dogs who are measuring each other up for a fight, walking slowly in circles, and watching for an advantage.

Like with parenting, distraction proved to be the best peacekeeping tool. Now with Brawny and Margit raising their voices, I needed to step in and quell the emotional overload fast.

"Let's go over the schedule one more time. Tomorrow we have Margit doing the Christmas Carolers. Wednesday the Crafty Cuties are coming here, and I'm teaching icosahedrons, the twenty-sided equilateral shapes with triangular faces. On Thursday, Brawny teaches crocheted jewelry. Friday, Laurel will demonstrate how to make a snowman luminaria. On Saturday, Clancy will create those cute spa kits, with the packaged soaps and handmade labels. Moving right along. Laurel? You're teaching the kids' class, Fantasy Jars, on Sunday, right?"

She nodded happily, which was good to see after she'd had such a scare with that cop. "I've already gotten the paper clay and pinned ideas to the display board. Got the poster paints ready, too. The kids will start the project on Sunday and come back during the week to finish it up."

"Or they can take it home," I reminded her.

"But if they come back, that means another crack at selling their parents craft supplies. Margit and I put together the coolest kids' craft baskets. They're in her garage," Laurel said, as her fingers tapped buttons on her smart phone. Passing the phone around, we saw photos of the baskets. They knocked my socks off.

"Wow," I said. "Good work! It's back to Rebekkah on Monday for Dodie's Turtle containers, and Margit will also teach a children's class on gingerbread men."

We turned toward the computer where Rebekkah held up a sample of the finished product, ultra-cute turtle containers.

"Um, can I ask a favor?" the young woman asked, her troubled face filling the screen.

"Shoot," I said, giving her the go-ahead.

"Dad is really down. He's missing Mom something fierce. Can he come with me to teach my class?"

My heart sank. This would be Horace's first holiday season without Dodie. While it's true that Hanukkah is *not* the Jewish form of Christmas, the holidays are still the holidays. There are family rituals that Jews develop in these dark winter months. For many, the holiday season is particularly difficult because it reminds them they are a religious minority. Dodie and Horace were such lovebirds. They did so much together and shared such a bond of friendship. I should have realized this would be hard for him. I wanted to kick myself for being so thoughtless.

"Of course he can!" I said, almost too quickly.

Margit removed her glasses and polished the lenses. "I remember how they would drive through town and look at the lights. They loved seeing the displays. Afterward, they would go home and have hot cider and donuts."

Rebekkah's voice broke as she said, "Apple cinnamon donuts. Mom used to make them. Dad would put on *Miracle on 34th Street*. They watched that and *Bell, Book, and Candle*. It was their tradition."

I vowed then and there to do something. I wasn't sure what or how, but I couldn't turn my back on Horace Goldfader. Not when he and Dodie had done so much for me.

Swallowing hard, I finished my list.

"On Tuesday, Brawny will make quilted eyeglass cases. That Wednesday, I'll teach the album-in-a-folder class twice, once to the Crafty Cuties. Then on Thursday, Margit will teach the dollhouse-in-a-ring binder twice, once to a group of moms whose daughters attend the same school and again to the general public. Back to Clancy, who will show folks how to make tiny books and convert them to earrings or necklaces. We end our twelve days with me teaching how to make a book garden."

By the time I finished the list, I was exhausted!

CHAPTER 28

The tension between Brawny and Margit continued to percolate during our staff meeting. Laurel acted cheerful, but I could tell she was concerned about being targeted by the cops. Who wouldn't be? The realization that Horace was hurting put a damper on my spirits. In short, my happy helpers had taken a hike, leaving me with a group of grumpy gnomes.

At noon, in walked Ester Field, red-eyed and sniffling.

"Ester!" I gave her a big hug. "We are all so sorry about what happened to your sister."

She bobbed her head and retrieved a tissue from her purse. Dabbing her eyes, she said, "I hope I haven't missed too much classwork. It's been difficult, as you might imagine. At least I was there with her at the end. Even though we lived in the same house, I've always worried that Eudora might slip away, and I wouldn't know she was dying."

My face registered my confusion.

Seeing my reaction, Ester explained, "Long ago, my sister and I had a fight. As a result, we divided the house in two sections. I got a bathroom and one bedroom; we shared the kitchen and the laundry room. Eudora had the rest of the place. Two bedrooms, a bathroom, a powder room, a living room, and a dining room. That's why I didn't always know what she was doing."

"That doesn't sound fair," I said.

"Oh, but it was. You see, our parents left the house to Eudora for the rest of her natural life. For me, it was a 'grace and favor' situation. I got to stay there by God's grace and because Eudora was doing me a favor. After the kids moved out, my husband left me. Up and disappeared. I'm basically indigent, but my sister gave me a roof over my head. Between that and the odds and ends of work I've done, I've managed to get by."

"What will happen to you now?" The words were out of my mouth before I could stop them.

"Since Eudora is dead, the house is mine. I'll probably take in a renter to help cover the costs. It's possible Eudora left me money, but I doubt it. She's more likely to have left it to charities or our distant cousins as a way of punishing me."

"Punishing you for what?"

Ester slid her purse off her shoulder and let it fall to the floor. I offered to hang up her winter coat, a tired woolen blend that smelled of hair spray. While I did, she pulled up a stool and leaned her elbows on the craft table where I was prepping the icosahedron class. Her movements spoke of heaviness, as though she dragged a boat's anchor from each limb.

"Eudora was supposed to live a charmed life.

She was always our parents' favorite. Her grades were outstanding, and she inherited our mother's good looks. But she fell in love with a guy who didn't return her affection. After he broke her heart, I got engaged to Billy Robinson. For a while, it seemed like Billy and I had everything. A good marriage. The house, the kids, the car. Meanwhile, Eudora entered the Monastery of the Visitation as a postulant. When she wasn't invited to become a novice, she was devastated. Totally distraught. She stayed on as a teacher, but her anger kept growing and growing. Finally, she was let go from the school. Our parents were devastated. That's when they decided to leave her the house."

"But your husband left you! Surely she knew how badly that must hurt! Why punish you?"

Ester's half-smile broke my heart. "No. To her way of thinking, Billy left because I did something wrong. The fact that I had kids and grandkids really galled her. Believe it or not, she used to like young people. That's one reason she wanted to become a Visitation nun; she wanted to serve others by being a teacher. That desire turned sour over the years. She grew to despise young people. She became more mean-spirited with each semester. Resentful. To be honest, she always was a bit of a bully. What she did to your Zentangle portfolio is an example. If she didn't get what she wanted, she made other people pay."

"She seemed to crave being the center of attention."

"Yes," Ester nodded, "and she could be perverse about getting it. That whole thing about not having a funeral service that included our friends? Her way of getting attention. Her way of striking at us from the grave. She wanted to deny our family the comfort of our support systems."

"And she did," I said.

"And she did."

"You are coming next week to the Zentangle class, aren't you? Bringing Caitlyn, too?"

Ester nodded. "It's our special outing together, Caitlyn's and mine. I wouldn't miss another one of your classes for the world."

I hesitated to ask the next question, but I had to. "What have they decided about the Demski Award?"

Ester sighed deeply and looked away from me. "They won't make a decision until after the holidays."

I gave Ester the only comfort I could, a hug.

CHAPTER 29

After Ester left, I remembered I had her sister's Zentangle supplies, so I sent her a text. She responded: *Not to worry. I'll collect them Wednesday.*

The rest of the day raced by. At lunch, I tried to eat the peanut butter and fruit tacos that Brawny had made for me, but I kept getting interrupted by customers. Clancy kept bringing the food to me with the admonition, "Eat!"

As much as I wanted to, our guests came first.

By one o'clock, both my feet were both swollen, so I had to stop and put them up. When Margit visited her podiatrist, she brought back a gel pack that fit over my tootsies like a cuff. We kept the cuff in the refrigerator especially for days like this. Knowing I couldn't go on much longer, I sank down into a chair, propped my legs up on two boxes, rolled the gel packs over my feet, and pretended to be Santa sitting in his chair at the mall. Our customers queued up, asked me questions, and walked away happy with the candy canes I passed out.

By two, I was back up and running here, there,

and everywhere. I shouldn't have been surprised by the rush of customers. Typically, craft stores are busiest early in December, when people think they'll make gifts for family and friends. Later in the month, crafters realize they'll never make that December 25th deadline, so they switch to buying supplies for their friends and family.

We had both types of customers. Those who were determined that this would be a handmade holiday, and those who figured that someone else could make like an elf and craft their own special keepsakes with the materials from Time in a Bottle. I was grateful to both, because every time the cash register rings, another angel gets her wings. *(I might be wrong about that, but I sure wanna believe that!)*

After she heard about my close examination of Clancy's undercarriage, Brawny insisted I go to the hospital. I told her I was fine. She pressed the matter until Margit said, "You know better than an EMT?"

Fortunately, it was two-thirty by then and Brawny had to leave to pick up the kids from school. Since it was the first night of Hannukah, Rebekkah had left early. I would have left shortly thereafter, but I got caught up waiting on a woman named Chloe Chang. She couldn't make up her mind about anything. Chloe took up two hours of my time, dithering. Should she buy her friend Jasmine the template in the shape of a honeycomb? Or the one like multiple raindrops? Should she give her daughter a series of Zentangle classes or knitting classes? Should she make a needlepoint belt or a key ring for her husband?

Most people work through these problems in private, but not Chloe. She needed an audience of one, me! Every decision demanded my input. If I tried to walk away, Chloe came trailing behind, yammering about the pros and cons.

I wanted to turn around and say, "I'm not that important! You can make these decisions yourself!"

Of course, I didn't.

But honestly, we weren't talking career moves. We were talking gifts. Most people, sensible people, are thrilled with whatever you get them. I always am! If they aren't, that says tons about them. Maybe they're too picky, too jaded, or too spoiled. My philosophy is that if you're going to pout about a gift that was chosen with love, you don't deserve the present.

"Chloe," I said, as I stopped so abruptly she nearly bumped into my back, "what does your husband do for a living? He's a doctor, isn't he?"

"Heart surgeon," she said. "Why?"

"Idle curiosity. I figured that if I knew more about him, I'd know whether the belt or the key ring was a better choice."

From across the aisle, Clancy stroked her nose, our signal that I was telling a whopper. We started using the coded message after Erik spent a morning at the store watching *Pinocchio*. Clancy was reminding me that lies would make my nose grow longer. As if!

Finally, I decided to be blunt. "Chloe, I'm sure your husband will love any handmade gift from you. If you'll excuse me, I need to get home so we can light the Hanukkah candles."

To my surprise, that worked. She wished me a happy holiday and took her purchase to the register.

I waved toodle-loo to my store and started for the parking lot.

"Not so fast," said Laurel. "I've been delegated to walk you to your car."

"I can—"

"Uh-uh, no, not happening," she said, as she pulled on her leather jacket. "After you."

CHAPTER 30

Erik wasn't entirely sure what the fuss was about. In fact, he couldn't even pronounce Hanukkah properly. When he tried, it came out, "Han-nooky."

"Actually," Detweiler whispered in my ear as he helped me take off my cape when I got home, "Han-nooky has a nice ring to it, don't you think?"

I turned several shades of red. Exactly as he expected! I gave him a playful nudge. "Cool it, mister. We've got company coming. By the way, we need to talk later."

"What about?" He nuzzled my neck.

"A little mishap I had and police harassment."

"A mishap? Are you okay?"

"Yes, and so is the baby. No big deal. I just slipped on the ice and fell. The bigger problem is police harassment."

"If you think this is police harassment," he said softly, "wait until you see what else I have planned."

I twisted in his arms so we could look each other in the eye. "Not of me, silly. Laurel. A cop stopped her for reckless driving on the way to work this morning. But she wasn't driving carelessly. The officer was from the Felton Police Department. Someone had anonymously called to tell them that a car matching hers with her license plate was driving erratically."

Those amazing bright green eyes of his darkened to evergreen. "Brad Oxemann. Behind the scenes. Manipulating."

"Laurel was really shook up."

"I can imagine." Detweiler let go of me as we heard a clatter from the dining room.

"I need to help Anya finish setting the table," I said. "Why don't you go and see if Brawny needs you to cut the brisket?"

Anya was digging around in the breakfront when I gave her a hug. Together we looked for serving utensils that hadn't been used since Thanksgiving. When we finished, Anya and I stepped back to admire the table. In the center stood the menorah, one of eight we owned. Each year we rotated them so that every menorah had at least one night of use. Tonight we stared at a ceramic version of Noah's ark, with animals as candle holders. Small pine branches from the Detweiler farm were spread around the candelabra. As a result, the animals looked like they were adrift in a raucous sea. The setting gave them an air of vulnerability. A reminder that most of our lives are lived in a small community where we're entirely interdependent. I thought of my co-workers back at the store and felt grateful to them.

"Perfect." Anya backed up from the finished table setting and clasped her hands to her chest.

For a heartbeat, she looked exactly like her father, George. She had his height, his pale coloring, his denim blue eyes, and his strong nose. A lump formed in my throat, as I stared at her. She was growing up so fast. As the years went by, would she remember her father?

Tears prickled behind my eyes. I gripped the back of a chair hard, and I might have burst into tears, except that Detweiler stepped out of the kitchen and gave Anya a big hug.

"Your father would have been proud of you," he said so softly that I almost didn't hear.

"Yeah," she replied in a husky voice. "I always miss him most at Hanukkah. He had such fun. He loved playing dreidel."

"You tried to teach me last year, and I'm hoping I can catch on this time."

She grinned and gave him a cheerful poke in the belly. "Ha, ha, ha. You won all the jelly beans last year and you know it. Are you looking for a rematch?"

"You bet!"

The two of them dissolved in giggles.

"What's funny? Who's laughing?" Erik came around the corner with the box of Hanukkah candles.

"They are, honey," I said. "Do you remember how many candles we need tonight? Come on, you can put them in the menorah."

Guiding those chubby little hands, I thought my heart would burst with joy. My prayer was simple: *Dear Lord, thank you for all that I have. May my children always be this happy."*

As if he heard me, my tiny passenger kicked

twice.

Just then, the doorbell rang.

"I'll get it," yelled Anya, tearing into the foyer.

The mood of the room shifted abruptly as Sheila Lowenstein Holmes, the mother of my late husband, stomped past the dining room—with a snarl on her face and booze on her breath.

CHAPTER 31

Robbie followed his wife, walking past where we were standing and into our kitchen. I didn't want to join them. Every cell in my body tingled with remembrance. I'd grown up in an alcoholic home, and I have no desire to relive those years. Lately, every time I've seen Sheila, she's been drinking.

Always irreverent, quick to speak her mind and not one to run from a fight, my mother-in-law is a handful even when she is sober. But a few drinks are all she needs to get totally out-of-control. She reminds me of a possum on a country road. Even if a car is heading toward her, and destruction is a sure thing, Sheila would rather bare her teeth and snarl than move to safety.

She has always liked her booze, but this spirit of indulgence has gone too far.

Sheila is putting her new marriage at risk. As Chief of Police for St. Louis County, Robbie needs to be a role model. Already, her behavior is eroding his reputation. Gossip about her drinking has spread to the surrounding municipalities that make up the metro St. Louis area.

Her addiction is also causing problems in their private lives. She's been escorted out of the country club more than once for belligerent behavior. I happen to know that just last month Robbie got a call from a local restaurateur to pick up his wife. Sheila had gotten soused during a girls' night out.

Luckily for us, Sheila didn't tip the bottle until after five p.m. That meant that in a pinch, I could trust her to pick up the kids after school. However, I knew from personal experience that it's always five o'clock somewhere! So far we'd been safe depending on her ability to hold off until dinner to have a cocktail, but I wasn't confident this restraint could last forever.

On the other hand, it wasn't my place to deal with her problem. I'd lived through childhood and adolescence as part of an alcoholic household. It was not an experience I cared to repeat. Sheila's drunken visits literally caused me to have nightmares. Detweiler has vowed to ban her from our home. But I begged him to let this problem play itself out. "At least let it go until after the holidays. We can manage until then."

Watching her wobble by us in a drunken haze, knowing she was intoxicated on the night of a sacred holiday, I wondered if waiting was a good decision. Maybe I'd been wrong.

Detweiler turned to stare at me. I could read his mind: *Should we ask her to leave immediately?*

I shook my head at him. Hanukkah is very important to Sheila. And to Anya. Surely my mother-in-law could control herself for one more night.

The doorbell rang. Anya ran out of the dining room. Erik streaked past, racing out of the family room. Detweiler smiled at me and said, "I'd better get the door." The slight squeak and the draft of cold air alerted me to the arrival of the elder Detweilers and their granddaughter, Emily. I pricked up my ears at Thelma's cheery voice and Louis's deep bass.

I made it to the foyer in time to greet Leighton Haversham and Lorraine Lauber as they came through the door.

"Aunt Lori, we're doing Han-nooky! There will be presents and games!" Erik tugged on her sleeve, and she leaned down to kiss him. Leighton beamed at Lorraine with joy.

A smile came to my lips, thinking of the love story unfolding in front of our eyes. From the moment they met, it seemed like Leighton and Lorraine were made for each other.

Even if my mother-in-law was tipsy, it was wonderful to have family and friends under one roof.

CHAPTER 32

After everyone took their seats, Anya moved to the head of the table, behind where Detweiler was sitting. "Mom? We have a surprise for you."

Detweiler stood up and motioned to Erik. The three exchanged glances, and then began, "*Baruch a-tah...*"

That prayer had never sounded as beautiful to me as when three of the people I loved most in this world chanted it together. As the ancient words joined our young family, Detweiler lit the tallest candle, the *shamus*, and handed it to Erik, who lit the first candle on the right. With Anya's help, he returned the *shamus* to its place of honor.

The glow warmed their faces, those visages I loved so much. I couldn't guess where they'd found the time to practice the blessing without my hearing, but that didn't matter. What mattered was that they'd performed this labor of love for my benefit. As we all joined them with a final "amen," I wiped tears that spilled down my face.

Across the table from me, Sheila used a tissue to dab her eyes. Even Robbie looked like he was fighting with his emotions. The Detweilers smiled approvingly, while Lorraine and Leighton wore expressions of pride.

Although I'd been raised Episcopalian, I'd agreed with George that Anya would grow up in the Jewish faith. I've never regretted that decision, as the addition of Judaism to my life has opened my mind to new ideas, and my heart to new loves. When George died, Sheila worried that I'd try to convert Anya to my native religion. The three of us sat down and had a good conversation with Rabbi Sarah. While some say that a person converts because her faith is weak, I disagreed—and Rabbi Sarah backed me up. Although I never formally converted, I acted like a convert. I felt as comfortable in temple as I had in church. To me, God is everywhere and in everything. The challenge isn't for God to find me, but for *me* to find God.

Sheila had scoffed at this. "If you were a true believer, you wouldn't be such a namby-pamby person. You would pick one faith and stick with it."

But Rabbi Sarah had said, "For some people, faith is like a gold liquid that takes the shape of whatever vessel it's poured into. I believe that's how it works for Kiki."

I couldn't have said it better.

Be that as it may, I understood why Sheila was worried. Having a Jewish granddaughter was important to her. Judaism was the link that kept Anya tethered to her father. If that link was broken, would his memory drift away, caught in the currents of time?

But the scene before us was proof that Anya

knew where she came from, and that even as Detweiler took up residence in her life, she was still George Lowenstein's daughter. A flame isn't diminished when it's used to light another candle. Instead of weakening my daughter's sense of self, sharing her faith gave her a chance to strengthen it by making her a role model.

As Anya returned to her seat, I rose to give her a big hug. "I'm so very, very proud of you."

"I know that!" She gave me a peck on the cheek. Everyone laughed at that.

The brisket Brawny had made (according to my recipe) was perfect. The potato kugel proved an excellent companion. Anya and Erik announced that they had tossed the greens for our salad. Wisely, because not everyone was a fan, they'd put artichoke hearts, tomatoes, green onions, carrots, hearts of palm, cucumber chunks, sliced onions, and diced red peppers in small bowls so each person could make his or her own mix. The Detweilers contributed a fruit salad, rolls, and a corn casserole. Sheila's maid, Linnea, had whipped up a spinach soufflé, green beans almondine, and a delectable apple cake to complete our feast.

Detweiler excused himself to pull challah fresh from the oven. Its fragrance made my mouth water.

Brawny set dishes of sliced apples at each end of the table, as she announced, "Anya and Erik picked these from—"

"From apple trees!" shouted Erik. "Aunt Lori, I climbed one!"

"You did?" She reached over to hug him and

plant a kiss on the top of that wild mane of curly hair. "Was it fun?"

"Yes!" said Erik. "We goed to Poppy and Meemaw's farm. They have cows and goats and horses and too many cats."

That observation caused a murmur of laughter.

Lori turned bright eyes on me. "Thank you," she mouthed a silent message of appreciation for bringing Erik into our lives.

"My pleasure," I said.

CHAPTER 33

A good meal can go a long way toward making folks congenial. Robbie and Sheila seemed to have put aside their earlier discord, and we enjoyed a wonderful meal. Brawny offered to make all of us coffee or tea to have with our dessert. Anya helped her. We were all enjoying slices of the apple cake when Leighton announced that he had exciting news. Setting his fork down, he said, "Lorraine has agreed to move in with me permanently. We're flying back to California tomorrow to pack up her house."

"My driver Orson can finally retire to Costa Rica," said Lorraine. "He's been wanting to move there for years."

"But we'll be back in time for Christmas," Leighton added hurriedly.

"Yes!" said Anya, doing a fist pump. Then she gave Emily a high-five.

"Woohooo!" yelled Erik, although I suspected he was mimicking his sister rather than really cognizant of what was happening.

"Isn't that great?" Anya turned to her brother. "Aunt Lori will live right next door!"

That he got.

"Yes!" he said, imitating his sister's fist pump.

I opened my mouth to correct Anya, to tell her that she should call Lorraine "Miss Lauber," but Lorraine caught my eye and put a finger to her lips. Her Mona Lisa smile told me to hold my tongue.

"Anya," she said, in a patrician voice, "thank you for calling me Aunt Lori. I hope you'll think of me as another auntie, because I'd like to be one to you."

"I'm glad it's okay with you, and I'm gladder still that you'll be here with us. Erik hated it when you left to go back to California. I did, too. Besides, Gracie and Petunia love playing with your dog Paolo. See? We'd all be miserable if you didn't stick around. You should be here with us. If you need anything, we can help you. That's what families do."

The Detweilers beamed at Anya approvingly.

My daughter. What a lovely young woman she was becoming! I had no idea how Anya knew that Lorraine was in such a bad way. For the most part, a casual onlooker would think she was fine, but once in a while, her lagging gait signaled that MS was destroying her motor skills. I suspected that she was often more tired than we knew, but she hid her fatigue by excusing herself and disappearing or saying, "I think I need a time out."

We never questioned her absences. Instead, we concentrated on enjoying her presence. Often she would suggest quiet activities, such as reading to Erik, rather than playing in a more rambunctious manner. She and Anya had long discussions about books and conservation, two topics they both enjoyed. Lorraine is a confirmed Anglophile, a lover of all things English, so she has told Anya about her many trips to the United Kingdom. This sort of personal experience broadens my daughter's horizons and whets her appetite for travel.

Someday, maybe, Anya and I will visit those places Lorraine speaks of with such fondness.

My daughter's pronouncement that we are a family struck a chord with all of us. Lorraine's smile trembled as she stared down at her plate. Leighton reached over and took her hand. They exchanged a glance, the type of intimate communication that's decipherable only to a universe of two. He squeezed her hand lightly. She took his in both of hers.

Clearing his throat, Leighton said, "Anya, do you know you're one of my favorite people? You and Erik. I might have forgotten to tell you that."

"No, you've shared that lots of times." My daughter giggled. "But *I* know your secret. We're your favorites because Petunia and Monroe like us. If we didn't pass their test, we wouldn't make your list!"

That brought a grin to all our faces. We all knew how fond Leighton was of his pets. His pug Petunia wouldn't hurt a flea, even if it was biting him, and he was scared of his own shadow. It had taken him forever to feel comfortable around us. He'd warmed up faster to Erik, probably because Anya had brokered the introduction.

Monroe could be cantankerous, but once you

learned what he liked (carrots, apples, and lumps of sugar) and where to scratch him (behind his ears and under his chin), you could win his affection. As long as you didn't wear diapers.

Or if your name wasn't Sheila. She and Monroe didn't get along. They were too much alike—cranky, opinionated and stubborn.

My mother-in-law had been uncharacter-istically quiet throughout the meal.

"That stupid donkey," she said in disgust.

Robbie glared at her.

Just that fast, the air in the room chilled to freezing.

I held my breath. By my reckoning, she'd had two full glasses of wine during our dinner.

Most people wouldn't have noticed, but it was enough to put me on high alert. Growing up in an alcoholic home, I'd come to dread family dinners. Especially around the holidays. What usually started as a civilized attempt at discourse, always ended with a shouting match. It had taken me years not to feel nervous when I sat down with a table full of people. The last thing I wanted was to baptize our new home in that sort of acrimonious vibe.

And yet, I could tell that Sheila was spoiling for a fight.

Fortunately, everyone ignored her.

Robbie turned to Lorraine and asked her how she was enjoying our cold Midwestern winter. Thelma chatted about quilting with Emily and Anya. Louis and Leighton talked about plants. Louis asked our neighbor if he'd like one of a new variety of apple trees that Louis had recently ordered for his family farm. "You can plant it yonder by the shed. That way Erik can continue his climbing career closer to home. Of course, the tree will need to settle in and grow a bit before then."

Taking advantage of the shifting mood, I suggested that the kids open their Hanukkah gifts. That met with unanimous approval.

Detweiler and I had purchased Kindle Fires for all three children. We had coordinated gift giving with Leighton, Lorraine, the Detweilers, and Brawny. They gave the children gift cards to Amazon.

Sheila and Robbie's presents were covers for the e-reader devices. Erik was a bit mystified about what he was holding, but once Anya explained it to him, his little fingers happily explored the world of online books. Emily was totally absorbed right away.

I was ready to suggest that Brawny and I clear the table when Detweiler surprised me by saying, "I have something for you, Kiki." Of course, I had a gift for him, too, but it wasn't the sort of present you discussed in front of other people.

"Mine to you is private," I said, feeling the warmth of a blush steal up my neck.

"Mine is public," he said, leaving his chair and dropping to one knee. From his pocket he pulled a small navy blue box. "I've asked you many times, and you've agreed, but I haven't asked you formally. Will you do me the honor of marrying me?"

My head spun. I couldn't move.

He opened the box to show me a beautiful diamond ring. I knew immediately that he'd purchased it from Mary Pillsbury, because the design was unique.

"Say yes! Say yes!" shouted Anya.

"Yes, yes, yes!" echoed Erik.

"Please, please, please!" yelled Emily.

A lump in my throat kept me from answering. My eyes filled with tears, and I couldn't see a thing except for the gleam of the diamond as it sparkled. The rainbow colors danced around the dining room. As I tried to reclaim my emotions, Detweiler reached for my left hand and slid the ring on my finger. It fit perfectly.

I threw my arms around Detweiler's neck, and inhaled the scent of him, soap and sandalwood, combined with a touch of male. "Oh!"

"Oh is not a yes." He pulled back from me, but he didn't turn loose of me entirely. "I'm waiting."

"Yes!" I said. "Of course I will!"

"Good," he said, "because I wasn't going to let you go until you said you would."

CHAPTER 34

I could feel Sheila's eyes on me. While everyone else rushed to congratulate us, she sat glued to her chair. The Detweilers hugged and kissed my husband-to-be and me.

Brawny brought out a bottle of champagne. Detweiler carefully popped the cork and poured a splash for me into a glass. Then he gave everyone a taste, allowing the kids just enough to wet their lips.

"To the happy couple," said Leighton. "May you have many, many years together!"

"To our new daughter," said Louis.

Instead of raising her glass, Sheila quaffed her drink and looked around for the rest of the bottle of wine that had been sitting at her end of the table.

It was gone. I suspected that Robbie had shifted it to the other end, because two bottles were now sitting in front of Lorraine. They hadn't been there before. We'd begun the dinner with a bottle at each end.

Pushing back her seat, Sheila leaned behind Robbie and motioned to Lorraine. "Hand me that wine."

Her rudeness shocked me.

"It's empty," Leighton said quickly. Too quickly, in fact.

"Kiki?" Sheila half-rose from her seat. "Where's more wine? You have to have another bottle somewhere in this big barn."

Considering that she lived in a house even bigger than ours, the remark came across as hopelessly snarky.

"Afraid not," said Detweiler. "Since Kiki's pregnant, neither of us are drinking. All we had were those two bottles of wine and this one of champagne. I bought it today to celebrate."

"Celebrate," Sheila echoed the word. Her mouth twisted in an ugly way.

"Congratulations again," said Robbie.

"Huh," said Sheila. "Twice a fool."

The words hit like a slap in the face.

Thelma's jaw dropped, and Louis reached over to take her hand. "I think we'd better get going. Tomorrow's a school day for Emily."

Anya looked up from her Kindle and stared at her grandmother, but Sheila didn't notice.

After we told the Detweilers goodbye, I expected Sheila and Robbie would want to leave, but to my surprise, Sheila seemed perfectly content at the dining room table.

"Kids? Why don't you take your presents into the living room," I said. "Anya, honey, would you help Erik load a book on his? Thank you, sweetheart."

My daughter hesitated. "Mom? Detweiler? Can you get married before the baby comes?"

"We'll talk about that later, honey." I wanted her out of the room, out of harm's way. My senses tingled. The air was charged, the atmosphere as electric as it gets before a storm. Sheila's energy shifted. I could guess what was coming. Those denim blue eyes so like Anya's had turned a deeper color, a cross between cobalt and navy.

I knew this scenario. It was as if I'd written a script. The pace, the intonations, the heightened responses were familiar to me. Sheila was drunk. All her disappointments were about to be spilled onto our table. Whatever was eating her—and I truly believed that something was causing her this angst—it had festered to a head. Any minute now, she was going to explode.

I didn't want my children to see the eruption.

Brawny hustled the kids out of the dining room. I was ever so grateful, because I couldn't move as fast as she did. After the busy day at the store, my feet had swollen to twice their normal size. With the burgeoning shape of my belly, scooting back my chair was a big production.

Brawny had no sooner shepherded Erik and Anya out of sight when Sheila tossed her damask napkin down on the table, the way a knight might have thrown down his gauntlet.

"So that's how it is. Robbie the Snitch warned you to lock up the booze, right?"

"Sheila, I promise you he's done no such thing." I kept my voice even.

"Whether you like it or not, I told you the truth," said Detweiler, getting to his feet. "Now, how about another cup of coffee? Anyone?"

"You're on his side! My darling husband," and

Sheila drew out the word, "has decided that I'm a lush. So he's acting like a Boy Scout. His goal is to dry me out, isn't it?"

She elbowed Robbie hard enough for him to wince.

This tangle of aggression and accusation had once been a part of my past. Sheila had invited me to dance, and the steps were achingly familiar. I should have kept my mouth shut, but I couldn't. My role was woven into those twisted strands of my DNA. "No, honest! It's because of the baby, Sheila. We don't keep—"

But she cut me off, pointing at Detweiler. "He's not pregnant. And your nanny isn't. Or so I presume."

"Sheila," said Detweiler, "we've only recently moved into this house. Until now, we've never had room to store booze. With Kiki being pregnant—"

"Knock it off," she turned on him. "How much has Robbie told you? That I got booted out of the country club? Those stuffy idiots wouldn't know a good time if it bit them on the backsides."

My blood pressure climbed in tandem with the pitch of her voice. How I hated this! Suddenly I felt sling-shotted back to my childhood. I knew what was happening, and I was powerless to stop it. I cowered in my chair.

Detweiler noticed. Even though we were both seated, he reached over and pulled me tightly to his chest. "Stop it, Sheila. I won't have it. Not here. Not now."

"You won't have what? Me telling the truth? What's the matter, Detweiler? You too accustomed to kissing up to your boss?"

Robbie stood up. Speaking to the top of Sheila's head, he said, "Time to go."

"I'll go when I'm good and ready."

"Mama Kiki?" Erik came running to me, holding up his Kindle. "Look! A book!"

"Yes, sweetheart," I said.

Brawny was two steps behind Erik.

Giving me an apologetic look, she swooped him up. "Let's go back into the other room, my wee lad. I want you to show me all the pages."

As she walked away, Robbie touched Sheila on her shoulder. "Sheila, it's time for us to head home."

"You aren't the boss of me," she said.

That awakened my slumbering adult-self. I didn't have to take this. Once upon a time, I had no choice. But now I did. My children didn't need to see or hear this nonsense – and I had the power to nip it in the bud.

I got to my feet. "Robbie is not the boss of you, Sheila. But I am, because this is *my* house. Those are *my* children in the other room, and these are *my* guests. Mine and Detweiler's. You have now officially overstayed your welcome. Robbie, please take your wife home."

CHAPTER 35

Detweiler escorted Robbie and Sheila to the door, pausing only long enough so the kids could tell them thanks and goodnight. Meanwhile, Leighton hopped up to help me clear the table.

"Let me do the heavy lifting," he said to me. "You need to conserve your energy."

"Sorry about that," I said, trying to avoid the expressions of pity on Leighton's and Lorraine's faces.

"Not to worry," said Lorraine.

"That's wonderful that you'll be here with us!" I hugged her gently. "Thank you for being so kind to Anya. We don't have a lot of family, and my mother isn't much of a grandmother, so your offer to be her 'Aunt Lori' means a lot."

"I could never have imagined that something so good could have come from my brother's death, but here we are. Now I have Leighton, a new home, a new dog, and a family. So much to celebrate this season!" She hugged me back, more tightly than I expected.

As Leighton took a load of stacked plates to the kitchen, Lorraine said, "Kiki, I couldn't be happier for you and your future husband."

Future husband. I liked the sound of those words.

Although we'd talked about getting married, Detweiler's romantic gesture still plucked my heartstrings. He was fully cognizant of what his proposal meant to me, because he knew that George had never formally proposed.

When I had told George Lowenstein that I was pregnant, he had done an about-face and walked away from me, leaving me standing in the middle of campus by my lonesome. Years later I'd learn that he spent that evening and the next with his old girlfriend, Roxanne, a prelude to telling her goodbye. Two days later, he showed up outside my dorm room. "I guess we need to get married," he'd said, simply. "I'll have to find you a ring."

"Is that what you want?" I had asked.

"Does it matter? I knocked you up. It's my baby. My responsibility. This is something I have to do."

Guilt had soiled our entire relationship, the way dirty water wicks its way up a clean towel. I felt indebted to George for bailing me out of a tough situation. He considered me a mistake he had to live with.

Later in our marriage, I uncovered a host of secrets my husband had kept, and I was forced to reconsider George's agenda. The truth was that George had married me because my pregnancy fulfilled one of his life goals. Our coming together had been a lucky accident, one that benefited him more than I knew.

Most importantly, George could face his dying

father and tell Harry Lowenstein he was going to have his much wanted grandchild. Secondly, George could make a clean break with Roxanne. Third, he could step into his father's role as the man of the family, guiding Sheila through the heartbreak of losing her husband to cancer.

Yes, in retrospect, George didn't do me any favors; I'd done him one.

Well, that wasn't true. He'd been a good father to Anya, and a good provider for our family. But he had allowed me to feel indebted to him. In fact, he'd fostered my feelings of inadequacy by calling our marriage (in private) "making the best out of a bad bargain."

I swore I'd never be in the same situation again. Then it happened. Last spring, Detweiler and I experienced what he laughingly called "equipment failure."

Just like that, I found myself pregnant and unmarried for the second time around.

Remembering how indebted I'd felt to George, I had told Detweiler that I wouldn't marry him until *after* the baby came. I never, ever wanted to feel like I'd forced myself on another man. I said all that, even though I felt like a jerk telling him "no" (especially after he had whooped with joy at the news).

In short, he'd had the exact opposite reaction as George Lowenstein.

No matter how many times Detweiler asked me to reconsider, I held firm to my "no." In the meantime, I had discovered yet another reason for turning down Detweiler's hand in marriage. It happened while Anya and I were getting fitted for our dresses to wear to Sheila's wedding. My daughter had gone into hysterics when she realized that a union between me and Detweiler would leave her as the last Lowenstein standing. What else could I do but promise Anya that I wouldn't marry Detweiler until after the baby came? Furthermore, I assured Anya that I wouldn't change my name.

That left Detweiler as the injured party. His dream of carrying on his family lineage had been kicked to the curb.

I felt trapped, pulled this way and that, between the two people I loved most in the world.

God bless Detweiler for being willing to compromise. He suggested to Anya that she and I could hyphenate our last names, adding Detweiler to Lowenstein. Sure it would be a mouthful, but really, who cared?

She promised to think on it.

His earnest desire to consider her needs began to soften the hard stance she'd taken.

Her incalcitrance further eroded, as my belly grew. Watching my body change, Anya had come to realize the practicalities involved with bringing a new life into the world. Accompanying me to my first sonogram, she had met her new brother at his most vulnerable. Seeing him so tiny and helpless on that screen, she learned that having a baby meant a whole host of responsibilities. When the receptionist handed me the bill for the office visit, Anya also recognized that having a baby was an expensive endeavor.

"Mom," she said, "if you married Detweiler, wouldn't his insurance pay for a lot of this?"

"Almost all of it."

My daughter is nothing if not practical.

"Then you two need to get married," she said, "and you need to do it fast."

CHAPTER 36

Later that evening after all our visitors had left, Detweiler and I finally had the chance to spend time sitting with the kids and admiring their Kindles. Erik loved the bright colors on the screen, and the fact he could switch from book to book. He stared at the images until his big brown eyes drooped with sleepiness.

"My wee bonnie lad is tuckered out." Brawny came from the kitchen where she'd started the dishwasher. She lifted the boy into her strong arms.

After she took Erik upstairs to bed, Anya turned to me and said, "I hate it when Gran has been drinking."

"I do, too."

Detweiler shook his head. "You know, Anya, most people don't realize how unattractive they are when they're drunk. It's a shame that Sheila can't see herself. She's always so particular about appearances. She'd be appalled."

My daughter nodded and came closer to me. "Can I see your ring, Mom?"

"Of course."

"Do you like it?" Detweiler asked Anya.

"Yes," said my daughter, "it's beautiful. Congratulations. I mean, I knew you two would get married, but this makes it official, doesn't it?"

"It certainly does," I said, holding up my hand so we could all enjoy the prismatic colors my diamond threw on the walls.

"Erik's in bed," said Brawny. This was the cue for Detweiler and me to go up and tuck him in.

Anya came upstairs with us. "I'm going to bed early," she said, giving us both a hug and a kiss.

"Are you feeling okay?" I pressed the back of my hand to her cheeks.

"Just tired," she said. "That's all."

Later that night, Detweiler and I were lying in our bed. He had his arms wrapped around me, as best he could, considering my humongous belly. I pressed my cheek against his chest and listened to the soft *lub-dub-lub-dub* of his heart.

"Thank you again for my ring. It's beautiful," I said to his sweet skin.

"You deserve a ring that reflects how lovely you are. Especially now that you're carrying our baby."

"Did Mary Pillsbury help you pick it out?"

"She designed it. You know, Mary. She's a perfectionist. But if you don't like it—"

"I love it," I said, interrupting him and pulling his head down so I could kiss his lips. "This was the best Han-nooky ever."

"Except for Sheila," he said with a sigh.

"Except for Sheila. She's really getting out of control."

"Fortunately, she's not our problem."

"Right," I said.

Why was I still worried about her?

CHAPTER 37

Tuesday, December 12...

It was heavenly waking up each morning to the smell of toast and coffee, even if I couldn't drink the caffeinated beverage.

Thank goodness for Brawny. Every day, she got up super early and started her routine. She was more than a nanny; she was a wonderful helper for our entire family.

Lorraine had insisted on paying Brawny's fees so the woman could stay with Erik and continue as a constant in his life. Seeing the bond between our son and his caregiver, Detweiler didn't have the heart to separate the two. Making a snap decision, he brought Brawny back with him from California.

I didn't know she was coming.

At first, I thought the ramrod straight woman dressed in a kilt and wearing a knife strapped inside a garter holding up her knee socks was some sort of a joke.

But Brawny quickly dispelled that notion. She proved to be invaluable. Not only did she take over most of the carpool responsibilities, she also did a lot of the cooking for us. Her needle art skills were the frosting on the cake!

Brawny had gone from school immediately into Special Forces. Five years later, she decided to act on her love of children. She left the military to attend the Norland College for Nannies. After three years of courses on child development, including food and nutrition, care and wellbeing, play and learning, as well as driving under hazardous conditions, she finished her dissertation on "Stress and the Young Child: Mitigating Factors, Intervention, and Character Building." Then she interviewed with Van Lauber and won the job as Erik's nanny.

The first sight of her in her kilt, white blouse, knee socks, and brogues usually caught people off-guard. More than one person asked me if she was "for real." But once I got used to her daily uniform, I found it a pleasant departure from our culture's casual dress. Simply put, Brawny looked elegant in a curiously old-fashioned way.

Not only was she dedicated, knowledgeable, and hardworking, Brawny also proved to be a worthy friend to us all.

Each morning she ran five miles with Detweiler, urging him to improve his time. Next they went into the basement where they had set up a gym. There she spurred him to working with heavier and heavier weights. "Thanks to her, I'm in the best shape of my life," Detweiler had told me.

After showering and changing, she would make us our breakfast. Because morning sickness has made this meal particularly unappealing to me, she routinely sets out a cup of Earl Grey tea and a plate full of toast.

"What do you call this thing?" I asked the morning after the first night of Hanukkah. I pointed at a silver gizmo that reminded me of a mail sorter with slots. Slices of toast stood at attention vertically, as if waiting for my inspection.

"A toast rack. I had me sister send me several. When you lot stack up your toast on plates, it traps the moisture between the slices, so they get all soggy. This keeps them crisp."

I nibbled an edge. "Gosh, you're right. This is wonderful. Isn't it great that Lorraine and Leighton are moving in together? I know you think the world of her."

"Aye, that I do," said Brawny. "'Tis all good, really it is, except..."

"Except?" I wondered.

"I'll miss Orson. He was in Special Forces, too, you know. A great man. He protected Miss Lorraine, while I watched over our wee lad. He'd do anything for her. Lay down his life for her. Certainly, he'd kill to keep her or the child safe. As I would."

"Wow." This was too intense for a breakfast conversation. I sipped my tea and tried to think it through. "So you're worried about her safety?"

"*Aye*. With great wealth comes great envy, and huge responsibilities. She's going back to tell Howard Thornton, her brother's attorney, that his services are no longer needed. I fear he won't take the news well." Her face grew fierce. "In fact I know he won't."

"Really?"

Detweiler had mentioned the attorney. We had agreed to sit down and talk after the holidays about the money that Gina had left for Erik. Given our move into the big house, and the demands of my store, Detweiler had decided our discussion could wait. I knew there was a trust fund that Van Lauber had set aside for Erik, but I didn't know the particulars, only that it was administered by an attorney, and that Lorraine had a lot of say in how it was released.

"Is this about Erik's inheritance?"

Brawny gave me a guarded smile. "Not my place to speak of such things."

"But you don't like this attorney, do you?"

"Try a smear of lemon curd on your toast," she suggested, pushing a small glass jar my way.

I did and moaned with joy.

"'Tis a rare treat to watch you eat," said Brawny, neatly changing the subject. "You get such pleasure from it."

"Except last night." I could hear my daughter rustling around upstairs. Anya was talking to Erik. His high piping voice sang out with excitement. He'd discovered new things he could do with his Kindle Fire.

Brawny sat down across the table from me. "*Aye*, Mrs. Holmes wasn't herself last night. She's usually such a fine lady."

"I worry that the kids were upset."

"I'll let you know if they mention it on the way to school. You do remember that Mrs. Holmes is picking them up after their classes to go to the mall and see Santa?"

I slapped my forehead. "I'd totally forgotten! You're prepping for your class this afternoon, right? The crocheted jewelry class?"

"That's right."

I finished my tea. "At least it's broad daylight and Sheila's sure to be sober. I don't think she indulges until after five."

"Let's hope not," said Brawny, clearing away my cup and saucer.

CHAPTER 38

Gracie, my harlequin Great Dane, rode along with me to the store. As usual, she sat with her rump on the passenger side seat and her front legs on the floor. On occasion, we'd pull up next to another car, and I'd see the driver do a double-take when coming face-to-face with her blocky black and white head. When the kids traveled with me, Gracie couldn't come because there wasn't enough room in the BMW. As a consequence, she missed our trips together. In particular, she missed going to Time in a Bottle and seeing Dodie Goldfader.

This would be our first holiday season without Dodie. All of us missed her terribly. I glanced over to see the tiny rubber band turtle I'd taped to my console in her honor. Dodie loved turtles of all shapes and sizes. The little toy had mysteriously shown up in the top drawer of her desk shortly after she passed. I took it as a sign from her. I moved the turtle into the car. When I drove alone, I could replay many of our conversations with my old boss. Sometimes I even mentally asked Dodie for help with a problem. The turtle served as her stand-in.

Although she'd never been overtly affectionate toward most animals, Dodie had a soft spot for Gracie. Often I'd pop into the back room to find her rubbing Gracie's ears while the dog sat in her playpen. Other times, I would discover Gracie lying on the floor next to Dodie's desk. The dog served as an ottoman for Dodie's feet.

When Dodie's cancer advanced to the point that it kept her from working, Gracie would wander into the office and search for her friend. On the day that Dodie died, the dog walked up to the big, black desk and howled pitifully. For weeks, she would stare at the desk and whine.

These days, Gracie would trot dutifully into the office, do a lap of the back room, and make a tour of the sales floor and needle arts room. Only then would she go to her doggy playpen and sink down onto her bed, a loud "oomph" that signaled her acceptance that Dodie wasn't here. Gracie would roll those sad brown eyes toward me and whimper. All I could do to comfort my dog was to reach down, pat her head, and commiserate. "I miss Dodie, too." I still couldn't bring myself to think of the room as "my" office. Most days I caught myself calling it "Dodie's office." Someday I'd have to do something to claim it as mine, but that was a task for the future.

I opened the computer screen and scanned the incoming emails. One immediately caught my attention.

It read: *Flying in on Friday. Restaurant holiday party is Saturday. Flying out Sunday early. Can we manage time together Friday night? – Cara Mia*

I typed a message back to her: *Pick you up at the airport Friday. Why not stay with us? We have room. Can't wait – Kiki*

I had just hit send when a loud knocking on the back door surprised me.

My sisters, Amanda and Catherine, shivered on the stoop. "I forgot my key," said Catherine.

"Come on in. I'll make you coffee or tea or hot chocolate."

"Coffee for me, black," said Amanda, pulling off her gray leather gloves. She was dressed for her job as a paralegal in a local law firm.

"Hot chocolate," said Catherine, taking the seat next to Amanda.

My sisters and I all look somewhat alike. We have curly hair, small noses, and blue-green eyes. But Catherine has copper-colored hair, mine is dishwater blond, and Amanda's is auburn. Catherine is the tallest, I'm the shortest, and Amanda is in between.

"Wow! Is that a diamond?" Catherine grabbed my hand to examine the ring more carefully. "He did a good job! Look at that, Mandy."

Amanda leaned over and admired the sparkler. "Nice. I guess this means you're going to marry him?"

"Absolutely," I said.

"Good deal," said Amanda. "The legalities of marriage are a good thing, most of the time."

After getting them their drinks, I poured hot water over the chamomile tea bag in my mug. "Not to mention the health insurance."

"Tell me about it," said Catherine. She was

marginally employed, working as many hours as possible at my store while temping at other businesses. That means that she and I both are without coverage. Amanda had terrific benefits, and she worried about the two of us.

"What's up?" I slid into a seat. "You want to know what to get the kids for Christmas?"

Amanda sighed. "If only it was that easy."

"It's Mom," said Catherine. "We hated to spring this on you, it being the holidays and all, but our mother is definitely losing her mind."

CHAPTER 39

I wasn't surprised that our mother was losing her grip on reality. The geriatric psychologist at the senior care center she attended had warned us that she was in poor mental health. "Borderline personality disorder. One of the most narcissistic people I've ever run across. Taken together, an extremely difficult woman. My condolences to all three of you. Having her for a mother couldn't have been easy."

"What else is new?" I asked my siblings.

"Let's see," said Amanda, pulling a sheet of paper out of her pocket. That's my sister. She's the Queen of Lists. "Last week, she put a frozen dinner in the microwave and set the timer for two hours."

Catherine didn't need a written reminder. "We found a pumpkin, a real gourd, stuffed into the back of her closet. Of course, it was rotten, and it had stunk up the place, not to mention the damage it did to the hardwood floor."

"Mom also turned on the oven and stuck her head inside to see if it was working. She singed her eyelashes," continued Amanda.

"There are her incessant calls asking what time it is," said Catherine.

Those I knew about, because she'd made them to me, as well.

"She's refusing to bathe herself," said Amanda, going back to her list. "Over the past fourteen days, she's taken exactly two showers, and that's because I stood over her and forced her to get under the water."

"Won't change her clothes, either," said Catherine. "She's been wearing the same peach-colored polyester pants suit for a week. The white blouse that goes with it is covered with food stains, but she insists it's clean."

Amanda raised an eyebrow at me. "Have you noticed how she limps? There's a reason for that. She couldn't find one of her bedroom slippers the other day, so she walked around the house barefoot. Her toenails had grown so long that they curved around the top of her toes."

"She's dropped four forks into the garbage disposal while it's running. She claims she was trying to poke the junk down, and that they slipped out of her grasp," said Amanda.

"Yesterday, she reached into the refrigerator, found a stick of butter, peeled back the paper, and ate it like a banana," said Catherine.

"Enough," I said. "I get it. What do you want me to do about it? If you've noticed, I'm not really in any shape to deal with one more thing. Especially if that 'thing' is our mother. Whatever the two of you choose, I'll go along with your decision."

Amanda stood up to pour herself another cup

of coffee. "I don't think we should do anything until after the holidays."

"I agree," said Catherine.

"So why are you here, sharing all this good news with me?" My mother had been nothing but hateful to me for most of my life. In my own head, I'd divorced myself from her. The idea of taking responsibility for her care sickened me. If they were suggesting that she come and live with us, they were barking up the wrong tree. No way was I inflicting that woman on my kids. *Uh-uh. It wasn't going to happen.*

"Because after the holidays, we all need to find Mom a new home," said Amanda.

"We thought you might have some resources that can help us. You seem to know a lot of people. Lawyers, doctors, real estate agents," said Catherine.

"That's true," I agreed. "But I don't know anybody who specializes in Arctic lots, and that's what we need, an ice floe. A big enough piece of ice so we can put Mom on it and push it out to sea."

CHAPTER 40

My sisters and I hugged goodbye. They pulled out as Margit's car pulled in. I was glad she hadn't overheard our conversation. It might upset her. Her own mother suffered from advanced Alzheimer's and wasn't doing well. That said, the assisted living facility that had taken Margit's mother might be a good match for our mother. I had visited more than once, and the place seemed very nice to me. I wondered what it cost. Amanda had put aside money from the sale of Mom's house expressly for a situation like this, but would it be enough?

Margit greeted me with her usual good cheer. In one hand was her knitting bag and in the other a double-level casserole dish. "Strudel in the top dish, sauerbraten and red cabbage in the bottom level. My Hanukkah gift to all of you, one day late."

My mouth watered at the appetizing smells. "This is fabulous. Thank you so much."

Margit waved away my appreciation. "Did you see the newspaper this morning?"

"No."

"A notice about Eudora Field's death appeared. They asked that donations be made to the heart fund."

"We can do that. How's the signed card for her family coming?"

"I think it's ready to be mailed." Margit sighed. "This is a bad time to lose a family member, *ja?*"

"Absolutely. Ester told me that she is free to live in the house until the end of her natural life. That's good. I was worried she'd be out on the streets."

Margit carefully hung up her wool coat. With great deliberation, she unwound the scarf around her neck and placed it along the collar of the jacket. The plaid of her coat was brown, mustard, bittersweet, and black. She'd fashioned a scarf in colors of sunburst orange and bittersweet with touches of black. When added to the coat, the effect was glorious. Her black gloves came off, and then the black tamoshanter.

"*Ja, Ill Wind bläst, die nicht gut.*"

"Translation, please."

"It's an ill wind that blows no good," said Margit with a sigh. "If you believe in karma, then you must clap your hands with joy. Eudora deserved what she got. Especially if you love animals."

"Why is that?"

"Lois Singer and I ran into each other at Schnucks a few months ago. I was looking at liverwurst when she told me about her cat, Tabby. He was an outdoor creature, no matter how much she tried to tame him. He'd been a stray who came to her door, you see."

I wished Margit would get to the point, but I knew there was nothing I could do to hurry her story along.

"Tabby kept using Eudora's flower bed as his litter box. Lois apologized repeatedly. She tried to keep him indoors, but he was a crafty devil. He slipped out one day and dug up a few vinca."

"Those grow back easily enough."

"Eudora was so, so angry. She banged on Lois's door. She said it was the last straw. Two days later, Lois found Tabby cold and stiff by her garage. He had been poisoned."

"She didn't!"

"*Ach*, I do not know and I cannot say for sure, but I think so. Lois is not the type to accuse a person wrongly." Margit removed her glasses and wiped her eyes. "That cat was everything to Lois. She has no other family. Tabby would come and go, but she would tell me such tales about that kitty. He brought her much joy. Much companionship."

"And Eudora killed him."

"*Ja,* I think so."

CHAPTER 41

Despite what Margit told me about Eudora being a cat killer, I was in a pretty good mood. Brawny had called to report that the kids didn't seem affected about the way Sheila had acted. Erik was his usual curious self. Anya a little quiet, but otherwise fine. The ever efficient Brawny had touched bases with my mother-in-law, and everything was a "go" for her to pick the kids up from school and take them to see Santa.

When the nanny showed up at the store several hours later, she and Margit were cordial to each other. The crocheted jewelry class wasn't scheduled until Thursday, but we'd listed Brawny as available for consultations with knitters all day today, helping them to finish up their projects. Indeed, almost as soon as I flipped the sign to OPEN, two women walked in, carrying their projects and needing one-on-one help.

After that, a steady flow of people came in, as this was the time of year when husbands visited our store to make purchases for their wives and daughters. Clancy had the day off, so Margit, Brawny, and I scampered like frantic squirrels.

Margit's adorable stockings proved invaluable. When a gift-giver mentioned a name, we looked up the number of the paper sock, pulled it down, and handed it over for perusal. The exact items and their costs were listed. That set my cash register to ringing merrily.

Laurel called shortly before noon to get our sandwich orders. I had her pick up a turkey on honey oatmeal bread for me from Subway, a nice change from my usual lunch at Bread Co.

The day went by quickly. For a Tuesday, we were unusually busy. Most of our customers were putting finishing touches on Christmas gifts. A couple needed help choosing colors of paper or the perfect embellishment. A few came in to show off their work before wrapping the gift and mailing it to the recipient.

The constant requests from our customers forced me to compartmentalize. My mother had her own little black box that I tied shut with a bright red ribbon. Sheila had a Tiffany blue box, tied with an elegant length of gold cord. Eudora's box was brown, the color of the earth to which she had returned. As for Brad Oxemann, his was white, gold, and navy, the colors of a police cruiser. With all these boxes securely taped shut, I could go about my work, concentrating on the needs of our guests.

My phone then buzzed with a message from Anya: *Call me! 9-1-1*

Fingers trembling, I did just that. My daughter didn't answer after fifteen rings.

That freaked me out so badly that I had to sink down in a chair and force myself to take long slow breaths. I called again.

"Mom?" Anya spoke in a whisper. "Someone needs to come and pick us up from Gran's house."

"Are you and Erik all right?"

"Yes. But instead of going straight to the mall, Gran drove us here. She said she'd forgotten her wallet. When we got here, she had a couple of drinks. I don't think she should drive."

"Do not under any circumstances get in that car with her," I said. "I'll be right there. If she gives you grief, tell her I'm on my way, got it?"

"Right." Anya hung up the phone.

CHAPTER 42

"Do you want me to handle it?" Brawny had been listening in.

"No. She's my mother-in-law and my problem. But Margit might need your help. Just promise that the two of you will get along." I stood up, trying to get my wits about me. Making a quick decision, I held out my hand. "Brawny, let's switch cars. I'll take Gracie along with me. Seeing her will take some of the sting out of coming home rather than visiting Santa."

"They're bound to be disappointed." She gave me the keys.

And why wouldn't they be? I thought to myself. After all, they'd been promised a visit with Santa. Instead, they were getting an afternoon with Tipsy, one of his merry elves!

"I'll walk you to the car," she said, as I threw on my cape, grabbed my purse, and snapped the leash on Gracie. Brawny took my elbow, guiding me through the slick parking lot. After I climbed behind the wheel, she loaded the dog into the Toyota Highlander.

But before she shut the door, she said, "Take a

second and calm down. The kids aren't going anywhere. They're safe. Anya is a smart young lady."

I squared my shoulders. "Right. Got it. Have a good class."

Margit stuck her head out the back door. "Sauerbraten!"

Brawny raced back, grabbed the double-decker trays of food, and put them on the floor in the back for me. Both women waved as I pulled out onto the busy street. It had taken a minor crisis to remind them that they were now on the same side…mine! The tangy fragrance of Margit's cooking started my mouth watering. I could almost taste the bite of the spicy cabbage and the savory richness of the pot roast marinated in vinegar and herbs.

Because most of the schools were in the process of letting out, the trip seemed to take forever. Of course, it didn't, but by the time I pulled into Sheila's driveway, I must have had a zillion conversations in my head with my mother-in-law. A few of them involved very salty language. Gracie picked up on my mood. She sat beside me in the passenger's seat and whined.

When I opened the driver's side, she bolted out behind me, before I could close her up in the door.

"Whatever," I muttered under my breath.

Gracie beat me to Sheila's front door and stood there, her tail wagging low and slowly.

Anya answered the doorbell. "Thank goodness you're here, Mom."

"Gracie? Sit. Stay," I told the big dog. She lowered her rump to the marble floor of Sheila's foyer obediently.

"Is that your mother?" Sheila's words were slurred. She came around the corner unsteadily. "Kiki? Why arc you here? We're going to see Santa today, remember? I decided to bring the kids here for a snack first."

"Really? I thought we were here because you forgot your wallet, Gran." Anya raised her eyebrows.

Gracie also regarded Sheila with suspicion. She perked up those uncropped ears of hers and stared at my mother-in-law.

"That, too." Sheila wobbled over to the door jam. Her eyes weren't focused, and the scent of alcohol coming from her was strong.

"There's been a change of plans." I tried to sound nonchalant.

Erik tootled his way down the hall, carrying in his hands a half-eaten, giant-sized Snickers bar. "Mama Kiki! We're going to see Santa." He threw himself at me, giving me a big hug.

The Snickers bar tossed me over the cliff. When she was sober, Sheila would have never given the boy a sugary treat. As a consequence of her indulgence, Erik would probably be bouncing off the walls until midnight. I lifted him up. "Change of plans, sweetie. We'll see Santa another day."

His tiny mouth puckered as a prelude to tears. But Anya rushed in to say, "Let's go home and play with our Kindles. How about if we get you a new book?"

Sheila wasn't ready to give in. "I said I'd take them to see Santa, and I plan to keep my promise," she said, angrily.

When I didn't respond fast enough, Sheila tugged at Erik's jacket. "Come on. You're going with me."

I opened my mouth to tell her to back off, but I never got the words out, because Gracie inserted herself Sheila and me. The Great Dane bared her teeth and growled at my mother-in-law.

Anya and I exchanged surprised looks. Gracie has never done anything like that. Not ever. But she'd made her position perfectly clear.

Tipsy or not, Sheila got the message. She took two steps backwards. "Fine. Have it your way, Kiki. Go ahead. Keep me from my grandkids. I would think after all I've done for them, you'd show me a little more gratitude."

CHAPTER 43

The kids had been fed and taken their baths by the time Brawny got home from the store. She bubbled over with excitement about how well the class had gone. "Margit did a brilliant job. Everyone loved the carolers."

Taking my lead, she didn't ask what happened with Sheila. I appreciated her sensitivity.

I had planned to review the situation with her and Detweiler at the same time when he got home later. The three of us could discuss what needed to be done next.

The phone rang while I was putting a load of clothes in the laundry. Even with my head inside the drum of the washer—fishing for one last sock—I could hear the shrill tone. I found the errant garment, tossed it into the dryer, got it running, and managed to pick up the phone before the caller hung up.

It was Robbie. He didn't even bother with a greeting.

"What happened today?" he asked peevishly. "I thought Sheila was going to take the kids to see Santa. When I came home, she refused to talk about it."

"She was supposed to take them to see Santa," I said, as I tucked the phone under my ear and kept piling dirty towels into the washer. "But after picking the kids up from school, she took them back to your house and knocked back a couple of drinks. Anya called me because she was worried about being in the car with her intoxicated grandmother behind the wheel. Thank goodness she did, because by the time I got there, Sheila was unsteady on her feet."

Robbie cursed. "I can't believe this! She and I got into it before and after our visit to your house. She promised me to cut back on the sauce. I have warned her repeatedly about drinking and driving, especially after that last episode."

"That last episode" referred to the fact that Sheila had been picked up once already for drinking and driving. Out of professional courtesy to Robbie, the police chief of that municipality had interceded, and Sheila hadn't been charged.

"I know she's not very happy with me," I said, "but that's tough. Until I am sure she's on the wagon, the kids aren't going anywhere with her. At least not when she's driving."

"I don't blame you."

"What are you going to do?"

"I haven't decided. I was going to wait until after the holidays and see if she settled down."

"You really think she will?" I sounded incredulous because I felt that way. "I sure don't."

"What are you suggesting, Kiki? That I lock her up and throw away the key? Retire early and babysit her?"

"I'm not suggesting anything, Robbie."

"Then what are you saying? What's your point?"

I blew out a sigh. I hadn't expected him to attack me, although I should have. It wasn't exactly surprising. I was an easy target. Sheila, not so much. "My point is that I doubt that Sheila is going to cut back. That's not how alcoholism works."

"Whoa. Wait just a minute, young lady. Your mother-in-law is not an alcoholic!"

"Yes, she is. When a person's use of alcohol interferes with her normal daily activities, she crosses a line. Sheila has always been a binge drinker. You know it, and I know it. But lately she's moved from occasional over-indulgence to daily drunkenness. If you don't call that alcoholism, I don't know what is!"

"We're not talking about a street bum here!"

"Alcoholics don't have to look like street bums. Some of them manage to hold responsible jobs. If you don't think that Sheila has a problem with alcohol, you're only fooling yourself, Robbie. That means she has two problems: you and the booze."

He hung up on me.

I didn't care.

Growing up, I had no choice but to lie about alcohol's impact on my family. Dad was "moody" and Mom was "not feeling well." Truth being, they were both drunk. Of course, my school counselors told me that I was wrong to consider my parents alcoholics. "Your parents come to all the PTA meetings. They are lovely people."

Yes, they seemed like "lovely people," because they limited themselves to a quick vodka and orange juice before going out in public. One drink managed to lubricate their wheels of social conduct. After they made it back home, the real fun began. Two drinks later, they started picking on each other. Three drinks and accusations were hurled. Four drinks and the yelling started. From that point on, it always felt like I was tap dancing on the Titanic. The ship was going down, down, down, no matter how fast I moved my feet.

No one had been there to protect me from the two drunks who lived in the same house with me. No one. I'd been all alone, trying to keep the peace, making up stories to tell my sisters, working frantically to pretend that nothing was wrong, so that my sisters didn't get freaked out.

It had taken tons and tons of energy.

Energy I didn't have these days.

Robbie could lie to himself all he wanted, but I knew the score. I'd seen this particular musical before, so I could skip the prelude. I wasn't interested in a reprise. My kids didn't need to deal with Sheila's drunkenness—and I didn't want to deal with it either.

CHAPTER 44

Detweiler came home and I kissed him and sent him upstairs to tell Anya and Erik goodnight. I considered accompanying him, but it would be my second climb in the last ten minutes, and I was exhausted. The conversation with Robbie had sapped the last of my energy. My first pregnancy had been when I was in college. Fourteen years later, the bodily changes seemed to slow me down more than I remembered.

Or maybe it was different back then because I had been so lonely in my marriage. Every second of that pregnancy felt like a gift, a reminder that soon I wouldn't be alone. I'd have my own child, a new beginning, a person of my own to love.

Today my attention was divided among two children, a man I loved, and a business I was buying. When I closed my eyes, I saw a fractured mirror, a mosaic of faces staring back at me, each with its own wants and needs. All demanding a portion of my scant energy.

I went into the living room and put my feet up on a hassock. The relief was immediate.

"Cup of tea?" asked Brawny.

She had this uncanny ability to disappear when I needed alone time and reappear when I needed help.

"Please?"

In a few minutes, she returned with a tray that held a cup of chamomile tea plus two shortbread cookies and a dollop of her fabulous lemon curd. I dug into the citrus dessert spread eagerly.

Detweiler joined us a few minutes later.

Usually Brawny would leave us alone, but this time she hesitated, her polite way of asking permission to stick around. Since we needed to talk about Sheila, I asked, "What's on your mind?"

Her response surprised me.

"A man called today from that church two blocks over. He wondered if they could borrow Monroe for their Christmas pageant. Since Leighton is out of town with Miss Lauber, I explained that I'd have to check with you."

"As long as he's cognizant of Monroe's shortcomings, it should be fine. Just remind him that anything wearing a diaper will set the donkey off."

"I'll mention that," said Brawny.

"Mama Kiki! Mama Kiki!" Erik called from the stairs.

"Hang on, Brawny. Let me go put him back to bed. Then we need to talk about this problem with Sheila," I said.

"I'll go up with you." Detweiler offered me a hand in getting up from the chair. "You might need help climbing the stairs."

He was right about that. Each step took an

inordinate amount of effort.

Snug in his bed, Erik looked at us with drowsy eyes. He clutched his Kindle tightly. "Daddy! Mama Kiki, I have old turtle, see?"

He turned around his e-reader to show us his new book. Because Anya owned a much-loved hardback copy of the same story, the narrative and pictures were familiar to me. I curled up next to him on one side, Detweiler took the other, and we read him several pages, but he fell asleep before we got to the end.

Since we were upstairs already, we rapped on Anya's door, and she bade us enter. My darling daughter was painting her nails. Detweiler gave her a careful hug and left us alone. I gave her a kiss and told her not to stay up too late. "I'll be checking on you before I go to bed."

"Aw, Mom, I'm not a baby. I can decide my own bedtime."

"Yes, sweetie, you probably can, but for a little while, you're still my baby girl. You don't mind too much if I look in on you?"

"Nope. I guess not." There followed a comma, not a period, so I waited for what she had to say next. "Are you real mad with Gran?"

"That's 'really' mad, and no, I'm not so much angry as concerned." I perched on the edge of her bed. "Anya, I'm sorry about what happened today. You know your grandmother isn't a bad person."

She turned shrewd eyes on me. "I know that. I love her. But I'm not going to get into a car with her after she's been drinking. Especially when we've got Erik with us. He's my little brother. That makes him my responsibility, right?"

"You absolutely did the right thing, but the fact that you had to make that decision illustrates one of the problems with alcoholics and addicts."

"What's that?"

"Because they aren't lucid enough to think clearly, other people wind up taking responsibility for them. Your grandmother promised me that she'd be the adult in charge, but she wasn't, was she? It's like if I ask you to watch Erik while I run out to the store, and you call a friend and don't pay attention to him. What if he gets hurt? See? What she's shown me is that I can't trust her. Not like I used to."

Anya nodded. "I get it."

"That makes me sad for all of us. It also puts me in a tough position. After what happened today, I have to be honest and tell her that I've lost faith in her. I'm sure she'll be angry with me. Again, it's about responsibility. If she had taken responsibility, we wouldn't be having this conversation. But since she's not acting responsibly, here we are. Denial is part of addiction. Sheila will deny that she wasn't in any shape to drive. She'll probably make me out to be the bad guy rather than accept her part in this. I'm okay with that. I know the drill. That's a coping strategy that addicts use to justify what they do. But here's what you need to know: You absolutely did the right thing. Now it's my turn. My priority is keeping the two of you safe. Sheila can fuss at me all she wants."

Detweiler and Brawny had waited at the top of the stairs for me to leave Anya's room. I had planned to discuss with them the problem with

Sheila, but I could barely keep my eyes open. Since all of us adults get up early, we decided to table our discussion until the next morning.

CHAPTER 45

Wednesday, December 13...

Over breakfast, Detweiler and Brawny agreed
with me that we could no longer trust Sheila to
pick up and drive the kids *anywhere*. With that
decided, we got out the schedule and made
adjustments to the carpooling routine. Detweiler
text-messaged his parents, who (like most farm
couples) are up and at 'em before daybreak. They
answered him immediately.

"Mom and Dad said they'd love to come over
and take Erik and Anya to the mall to see Santa.
Actually, I think Mom wanted to take them all
along, but she felt like Sheila had first dibs," said
Detweiler.

"That's good news." I marked on the calendar
that they'd do pickup carpool duty that day.

"I think they'll take them to dinner at the mall,
too. But I reminded them to check with Anya to
see how much homework she has, so they can get
her back at a reasonable hour."

That segued nicely into me relaying my
conversation with Anya about Sheila's
irresponsible behavior. I also shared Robbie's

accusation that I was unfairly labeling Sheila an alcoholic. "I sure hope Robbie won't take this out on you at work. He was really ticked off at me."

Detweiler shook his head. "He's too professional for that. Whatever he chooses to believe, Sheila has a problem. On some level, he already knows that. Our children's safety has to come first. He might disagree with labeling Sheila, but he already realizes there's a problem. I could see it on his face when they were here for Hanukkah. He would look at her and look away, as if it pained him to watch her. I can't blame the guy. I mean, come on! Sheila was already three sheets to the wind by the time they arrived. Then she helped herself to four more glasses of wine."

"Four? I only saw her take two," I said.

"I was sitting right next to her. She drained the bottle, Kiki."

Throughout this discussion, Brawny had done more listening than talking. I liked how respectful she was of our roles as parents. Although she had a formal education in child-rearing, she never pushed her agenda on us. We were always in charge. However, if she thought we were making a big mistake, she would diplomatically share her insights and leave the final decision to us.

"I will watch the children carefully to see if this causes any problems for them. I don't think it will. Anya absolutely did the right thing. More and more each day, Erik turns to her as his big sister. You should be very proud. She's a wonderful young woman."

That made me happy. Maybe this dark cloud had a silver lining. Sheila's misbehavior was intensifying the bond between Anya and Erik. The arrival of our baby would change our family dynamics yet again. Over the past months, I'd read everything I could on sibling rivalry and the impact an infant made on the family system. There was a good likelihood that both Erik and Anya would regress as they saw the attention a baby garnered. But a setback like that would be only temporary.

One way or another we'd muddle through the changes.

That said, Anya's willingness to step into the role of big sister would make things much, much easier on all of us. With that happy thought cheering me, Gracie and I headed for work.

Time in a Bottle had long been a haven for me. Years ago, I discovered scrapbooking through an article in a magazine. Soon after, I started coming to this store to learn more about the hobby. Like a lot of other people, it didn't take long for me to become addicted to creating family stories on paper.

An unkind person would point out that my pages told lies, because they focused only on the happy moments in my marriage to George Lowenstein. I prefer to think that my layouts featured selective memories.

After George died and left me penniless, Dodie offered me a job, a way to keep a roof over our heads (mine and Anya's) and to put food on the table. Once I came to work here, I decided to become Dodie's *best* employee. It was a struggle but I succeeded. When Dodie learned she had terminal cancer, she and Horace offered to sell me the store on contract. I became the store's majority owner. Margit also has a small piece of the pie.

To me, Time in a Bottle is more than the place where I work. It represents my journey from an unskilled, soccer mom to a highly motivated entrepreneur.

The sight of the cheery store sign, a bottle full of watches, always sends my heart leaping around in my chest. But today, a corresponding glance at the frozen surface of the parking lot caused a different sort of accelerated heartbeats. I did not want a repeat of my earlier "under the undercarriage" adventure. Shuffling my feet slowly over the slick pavement, I held onto Gracie for balance.

Gingerly, we made it to the back door. My troubles weren't over, however, because the lock on the back door refused to open. This happens a lot in the Midwest, where precipitation gets blown into lock mechanisms and later freezes. I huffed hot air on the metal. After what seemed like an eternity, I was able to finally open the door.

Clancy came along a few moments later. The coffee pot was perking, scenting the air with the rich fragrance of her favorite hazelnut brew. Even though I really, really wanted a cup of coffee, I settled for wrapping my cold hands around a nice mug of peppermint tea.

With great care, she took off her black cashmere coat and hung it on our coat rack. Her pink scarf followed. Last of all, she removed her black leather gloves, one finger at a time.

"I know you don't want to hear all this, having just moved into Leighton's house and trying to get ready for Christmas," said Clancy, pouring herself a cup of coffee. "But I have a problem. Actually a couple of problems, and we need to discuss them."

"Okay."

Clancy rarely comes to me with a problem. She's more often the person who offers a solution. So this sideways introduction had me worried.

"If we're lucky, your baby won't come early. If we're lucky. But even if little whose-he-what-sis waits until his appointed due date, we both know that January is prime time for ice storms. I'm worried about making the drive here from Illinois. It seems like 40 is always undergoing road construction."

"That's true. I don't think I've ever driven that east-west route and not seen orange cones somewhere along the pavement."

"That's got me worried. I've been giving this a lot of thought. There's really no reason for me to keep the house in Illinois. I wanted it at first because when Lawrence left me, I wasn't about to let him and his baby mama move into the place where I'd raised my children. But more and more the place doesn't suit me. I've decided to put it on the market. But even after it sells, I can't turn around and buy another place with the money. That house is my nest egg. I'll need the money to supplement my income."

"I'm sorry—" I started to apologize for how little I paid her.

She waved away my concern. "Forget it. This job saved my sanity. You're paying me as much as you can. Here's my point. To buy something in

Missouri, I'll need to sell my mother's house and borrow money from her. I still don't have enough credit as a single woman to approach a bank and get a reasonable loan. My brother has agreed that I can pay the money I borrow back to my mother's estate when she dies, because I have a life insurance policy on her."

I didn't even know she had a brother. That surprised me. I had thought she was an only child. I sipped my tea and said, "That means that my mother and sisters need to move out of the house in U City."

"Right, but not immediately. My real estate agent says that nothing will sell until the spring."

"That might actually be a blessing in disguise." I told Clancy about my mother's deteriorating mental health. "Rather than tell her that she has to relocate, we can explain that the house is being sold."

"You realize, of course, that you're talking like a rational person. Your mother won't react like a rational person. That's not how this goes."

"Yup, I know. But even so, it'll take some of the pressure off of my sisters. Right now they're fighting all sorts of guilt. Amanda especially."

Clancy sighed and shook her head. "Tell me about it. You know what I've been through with my mother, and what Margit's going through with hers."

"The joy of being a caregiver."

"I much prefer the joy of the being a gift giver. Buy it, wrap it, give it, and be done with it."

"Right. Like we've got a choice. Women live longer than men, so we're stuck taking care of our aging mothers. That's the new normal for our generation. That reminds me. Speaking of yuletide joys," and I told her how Sheila's drinking had spiraled out of control.

"You knew this was coming. Thank goodness you talked to Anya about not getting in the car with a person who shouldn't be driving. This little drama should make for an interesting Christmas at your house. But even if Sheila is a real pill, I envy you."

"How so?"

"My ex is taking my children on an all expenses paid cruise for Christmas. I'll be celebrating by myself."

"Then come to our house. You can unwrap presents with us. What can I get you? I've been meaning to ask."

"Something tall, dark, and handsome. Preferably employed. Five to ten years younger than *moi*, with a hankering for a cougar."

"Hmmm. That might be tough to wrap. Would you settle for a bow on top?"

CHAPTER 46

My quip caused her to laugh.

We were still chuckling when we heard a brisk knocking at the back door. Clancy was closer, and more mobile, so she hopped up and answered it.

Standing on the threshold was a man. Tall, dark, handsome, and a little younger than Clancy.

"Wow," she said. "Santa sure works fast these days."

"I'll say." I blinked in surprise.

Our guest looked from one of us to the other with an expression of confusion on his face. "Mrs. Lowenstein?"

"I'm Kiki Lowenstein," I struggled to my feet. Noticing how big I was, the man patted the air to encourage me to stay seated.

"Detective Raoul Vasquez, Felton Police," he said, extending a hand for a shake. "Homicide division." Then he pulled up a chair of his own and sat down beside me at the table.

"I'm Kiki Lowenstein, and this is Clancy Whitehead. How can I help?"

Clancy interrupted, "Before you get started, would you like a cup of coffee? It's fresh. How do you take it?"

"Black. Thanks, Mrs. Whitehead." The detective looked her over, up and down. Clearly, he liked what he saw. Clancy could easily play Jackie Kennedy in a movie. She has the same classic features, the wide eyes and strong jaw. Her dark hair is worn in a classic pageboy, the perfect foil for her simple but stunning wardrobe. Today she wore a cream-colored crocheted sweater over a matching ivory top. Her tailored brown slacks and alligator shoes finished the outfit perfectly, but the real touch of style came from the thick gold necklace and matching bracelets she'd added.

"It's Ms. Whitehead, and you can call me Clancy. I'm divorced," she said, before stopping abruptly. It wasn't like her to volunteer personal information. Especially to someone she'd just met. A soft pink blush crept up her neck.

Boy, oh, boy. This guy really caught her attention!

"This is an unofficial visit," said Vasquez, staring back at her. "I was hoping you could provide a few details, Mrs. Lowenstein, about the death of Eudora Field."

"I'll help in any way that I can."

"Kiki is very good at things like this. She just got engaged to Detective Chad Detweiler," said Clancy, as she carefully placed a steaming cup in front of Vasquez.

"Then congratulations are in order," said Vasquez. "He's a good man. I've worked with him on Major Case Squad projects."

"Thank you," I said. As he reached for his coffee cup, I noticed he wasn't wearing a wedding ring. So far, so good. Santa's elves were working overtime! Then it hit me. "Wait a minute. You're from *homicide*. Eudora died of natural causes. A heart attack."

"Right. However, we have a witness who claims she was frightened to death. Our witness says that Miss Field was startled by someone or something right before she suffered her heart attack. Is that what you saw?"

"Brad Oxemann," I said, spitting out the name like I'd bitten into a bad pistachio nut. "He's your witness, right? He wasn't even in the room when Eudora grabbed at her chest and slumped over!"

"You know Mr. Oxemann?" Vasquez had long dark eyelashes fringing chocolate irises. His name suggested that he was Hispanic, and his coloring was in concert with that impression.

I explained to him about Brad Oxemann being Laurel's stalker. "I've heard that Brad's been rejected for the police academy because of his unsuitable personality. I am not surprised. That guy is trouble. Gives me the creeps."

Vasquez stared down into his cup. "Very interesting. However, I still need to ask you a few questions."

"Fire away."

"Tell me what you saw and heard leading up to the incident with Miss Field."

I did as he asked, and ended by pointing out, "No one was sitting next to her. All her classmates were ticked at her, so they sat clear across the room."

"Why were the other women upset with her?"

Oops. I hadn't meant to spill the beans about

Eudora's misbehavior at the Demski Awards.

I told him how Eudora had knocked over Caitlyn's winning entry. "But that doesn't mean she won't get the Demski scholarship," I was quick to add. "The board will meet in January to decide what to do."

Vasquez's face didn't give away his thoughts, as he jotted a note to himself in a small leather notebook.

Classy guy. Most of the cops I knew used Steno pads, but not Vasquez.

"Anyone else have reason to want to see Miss Field dead?"

I told him about the incident with Lois Singer's cat.

"What about Miss Laurel Wilkins? We've heard she held a grudge against Eudora Field."

"You're talking about the SAT situation?" I went over what I'd learned from Laurel. "You have to understand that Laurel is the sweetest person in the world. She never holds a grudge. Ever."

Clancy had been leaning against the counter, listening in as Vasquez interviewed me. "Actually, getting caught cheating on the SAT is no big deal. Do you know what they do when that happens?"

Neither the detective nor I had an answer.

"They make the student take the test over, free of charge. Since most students do better the more often they take the test, I should think that Laurel would have been appreciative, not vengeful."

To that Vasquez cocked an eyebrow. "You know this because?"

"I taught high school. Years ago."

"Couldn't possibly have been that long ago."

She blushed again.

"I don't get it," I said. "If Eudora died of a heart attack, why are you paying attention to what Brad Oxemann says? He's clearly a cop wannabe. Isn't this an incredible waste of your time and resources?"

A smile flickered across Vasquez's face. "It would seem so, wouldn't it?"

"Then there aren't any signs of foul play."

He stared at me.

"You can still find a motive. There are plenty of those. And a lot of us had opportunity, but the means of death is still natural causes, right?" I was more than a little hyped because I felt like I'd betrayed two of the Crafty Cuties by blabbing about the dead cat and the Demski Award. Fortunately, I'd stopped myself before telling Vasquez what I knew about Ester inheriting the house she had shared with Eudora.

Detective Vasquez stared at me, thoughtfully, but said nothing.

"Kiki?" Clancy pinched the bridge of her nose, the way she does when she's getting a migraine. "You've heard people say that someone was scared to death? If Eudora Field had a dicey heart, the means could have been something incredibly subtle. Something that would trigger her distress, but have no impact on anyone else. I used to work with a teacher, an older man who had served in World War II on a ship out in the Pacific Ocean. One day a student came to school wearing a shirt with a Kamikaze symbol on it. That brought back so many terrible memories for my colleague that he had a minor heart attack on the spot. Of course, the student had no idea that his choice of clothes would cause so much anguish."

"You have to be kidding me," I said, making a little pooh-pooh gesture with my hands.

"Not really. Actually Clancy is right on the money." Vasquez smiled at her.

CHAPTER 47

I thought Clancy was going to start drooling. She was that taken with Detective Vasquez. From the surreptitious looks he sent her way, the feeling seemed to be mutual.

"I might need to stop back by and ask a few more questions," he said, as he got to his feet.

"Clancy? Could you give the detective a business card with our contact info on it?"

While she retrieved a card, I explained, "You're welcome anytime. Clancy's my right hand. She knows everything about our schedule. She's in charge of all our customer information."

Clancy shot me a grateful smile as she told him, "My cell phone number is right here. If you need me just whistle."

That brought a huge grin to the detective's face, and more blushes to hers.

After he left, I wanted to say something, but I didn't in case my taking notice might scare her off. In that way, Clancy's like a cat that's skittish. If you wait, she'll come around. If you push her, she'll hide under the sofa.

Instead of reviewing the visit, she and I got

busy double-checking the supplies for my icasohedron class.

Since this was one of our Twelve Days of Christmas Crafting Spectacular classes, I'd turned the twenty-sided shape into a tree ornament. My crafters could make theirs in red, green, or white paper. Using metallic or colored pens, they could tangle on all or just a few of the twenty triangles. The addition of glitter or sequins would add another touch of dazzle.

As the morning wore on, the number of customers through the front door grew by leaps and bounds. At twelve forty-five, I realized I hadn't eaten lunch. Ducking into the back room, I gulped down a tuna sandwich. Laurel's shift started at one, and we barely had time to exchange greetings before we were racing around like wild horses on the sales floor. Around three, activity slowed down enough for me to tell Laurel about Detective Vasquez and his visit while Clancy finally grabbed a bite of food.

"What on earth is Brad Oxemann trying to do?"

"Act like a big man. But mainly he's wasting everyone's time. I'm sure the Felton police have more important crimes to solve than a 'pretend' murder."

At three-twenty, Thelma Detweiler called to say that she and Louis had the children in the car. "We're on our way to see Santa! I'll be sure to tell him that you've been a good girl this year, Kiki!"

I loved Detweiler's parents.

Close to five, the Crafty Cuties began to file in. Lois presented me with a couple loaves of banana zucchini bread. "This loaf's for you, because I make it with bran, and you need the fiber being pregnant. The other's for us to share as a group. That is, if everyone trusts that I'm not poisoning them."

"Why would they think that?"

She shrugged. "I guess one of the Felton detectives has been snooping around, asking questions about Eudora's death. He had tons of questions for me."

"He came by, but as far as I know, Eudora died of natural causes. He didn't say anything to the contrary."

"It's that Brad Oxemann," said Marvela, poking her head between us. I hadn't seen Marvela come in. "He's trying to stir things up. He told the detective that Eudora cost my daughter Beth her spot on the girls' volleyball team."

"Really?" I shouldn't have been so interested, but I was.

Marvela fluttered her hands around her face. "Such a long time ago. Beth was hoping to get a volleyball scholarship to college, but she came down with the flu in the middle of the term. Eudora forced her to take the mid-term Latin exam on her first day back. Naturally, Beth flunked it. Then Eudora refused to let her re-take the test. She said that Beth should have been keeping up with her studies. The failing grade brought down Beth's average, because she'd already been having trouble with Latin. As a result, Beth lost her spot on the volleyball team and her chance for a scholarship. Eudora could certainly have handled things differently. She knew what was at stake."

"Geez. Eudora caused problems for a lot of people, didn't she? She killed Lois's cat. She ruined Caitlyn's project. Eudora accused Laurel of cheating. And she caused your daughter an opportunity to get a scholarship," as I spoke, I held up fingers to enumerate all the reasons people might want Eudora dead.

"Don't forget, she made Ester's life miserable," Marvela added.

"How so?"

"Eudora never let Ester forget that she'd be out on the streets if she hadn't taken her in. That woman made Ester's life a living you-know-what. For someone who wanted to be a nun, Eudora could sure be unforgiving."

"Unforgiving?" echoed Cecily Kelly, in her British accent. "She was downright horrid."

CHAPTER 48

"I have my own Eudora story. My husband is English, through and through," explained Cecily. She'd just walked through the door and hadn't even taken off her scarf, but she was clearly eager to talk. "Peter loves to garden, and he especially loves his roses. Over the years, he's collected several dozen that are unique. Some have been gifts from friends who grow hybrids. You can't buy them anywhere."

Marvela laughed, "But Eudora didn't believe that, did she?"

"No, she didn't," said Cecily, slowly removing her coat. "Eudora was green with envy when she looked at our garden, but she refused to believe that the flowers grew the way they did because Peter put so much time into them! She even told me to my face that she thought he was obsessed. I explained that those roses were his passion."

Lois shook her head. "I remember one morning I was out in my backyard, and I looked over to see Eudora clipping roses from Peter's bushes."

"I caught her at it, too," said Cecily. "I asked her many times to quit. In particular, I asked that she leave alone those flowers that were special hybrids. After all, Peter deserved the chance to enjoy those in full bloom. But Eudora made a nasty comment about pride going before a fall. She even had the nerve to tell me that Peter's love for his garden was a sin."

"What happened?" I asked.

"They all died," said Cecily, quietly. "Every last one of them. We suspect that she poured Round-Up on them."

"That's exactly what she did," said Lois. "I saw her putting empty blue canisters into the recycling bin. I didn't know what they were at first, but after your flowers died, I looked up the container online."

Our conversation stopped abruptly as Caitlyn and Ester walked in.

Although we all tried to act like nothing happened, I'm sure we must have had guilty expressions on our faces. There's a certain cadence to a natural discussion, and after we'd been caught talking about Eudora, that rhythm had been interrupted.

"Good," I said, in an overly cheerful voice, "we're all here. Wait until you see the special treat I have for you. We're going to make an icosahedron!"

"A what?" Caitlyn took a seat at the table and handed me a beautiful gift. "These are for you, Kiki."

I eagerly tore off the wrapping paper to find a box of chocolate covered cherries. "Goodie! We can share these at the break. There's also zucchini banana bread—"

"I brought chocolate-covered pretzels," said Marvela.

Not to be outdone, Cecily reached into her purse and hauled out a tin of shortbread cookies.

"What we have here is a surfeit of riches. Margit made slow cooker monkey turtle bread. Can you smell the caramel and chocolate?" I asked.

As the class started, Clancy and Laurel came over to join us. They wanted to see us turn flat pieces of paper into stunning ornaments.

"I think these are really neat," said Clancy. "Wouldn't a half dozen of them look great stacked in a wicker basket with a red ribbon around it?"

Laurel held up a white one I'd decorated with gold metallic ink as highlights. "Or you could trim a tree with these instead of using those blown glass balls. If you had a cat, that would be safer for the animal. No breakage."

The next hour passed happily as we worked on the crafts. I did as much teaching as I could from a seated position, knowing that I'd be teaching a second session at seven.

"Time for a break," I said. "Get up, stretch your legs, and sample some of the yummy treats we have on the food table."

The front door flew open, and my mother-in-law stalked in.

CHAPTER 49

"How could you!" Sheila shrieked at me. "Instead of letting *me* take the children to the mall, you let the Detweilers take them!"

Her wild demeanor was totally at odds with her carefully put together look. She had on a beautiful Burberry coat trimmed with black fox around the collar. Red gloves picked up the same color in the lining. Because she didn't have her coat buttoned up, we could see her bright red turtleneck, black skirt, and black boots. Every inch an elegant woman, except for the way her face was twisted with rage.

Out of the corner of my eye, I saw Clancy backing away from the scene my mother-in-law was making. I also noticed that my friend had her cell phone in her hands and was frantically punching buttons. I could only hope she was dialing Robbie Holmes.

"Sheila, calm down."

"I will not!" She waved her cell phone at me. "Anya sent me the picture of her and Erik! See?"

The screen showed Erik on Santa's lap. His smile was forced, a little fearful, like it often is with kids his age. I could see he was holding Anya's hand, causing her to lean in toward the man playing the jolly old elf.

"Looks like they're having fun," I said, trying to distract Sheila. To change her mood. Anything to avoid the train wreck that was happening right here, right now, in my store.

"Fun? Of course, they're having fun! They're both there. Erik's on Santa's lap! Anya's right beside him! Do you know where they are? They're at Frontenac in front of all my friends! Do you have any idea how humiliating this is? Why not just thrust a dagger through my heart?"

All the Crafty Cuties were staring at us. Laurel and Clancy were staring at us, too. But my friends demonstrated a sense of solidarity with me because of the way they were positioned, with arms crossed over their chests like two tin soldiers. Clancy took a step forward, but I shook my head at her.

Sheila was my problem. *Mine.*

I tried to take my mother-in-law by the arm. "Let's go talk about this in the back, okay?"

"It is not okay. Not at all. You're not going to get away with this. You can't toss me aside like a used piece of wrapping paper. Not when I've done so much for you! I still pay for Anya's tuition. I'm the one who got your son into CALA. I've helped you in every way I can, and this is how you thank me? By telling me I can't take my grandchildren to see Santa? Or have things changed now that Erik's here? Now that you're expecting a baby?"

That really ticked me off. She'd conveniently forgotten a part of our history. The part where she had tried to have Anya taken away from me by child welfare authorities. "Sheila, this isn't about keeping you away from Erik and Anya, and you know it."

"I don't know anything of the kind! I volunteered to pick up your children, just like I've been doing with Anya for years, but that isn't good enough for you. Not anymore. Now that you're engaged, you've dumped me. You've got a new family."

The women behind me shuffled their feet and tried to chat about the treats on the food table. Laurel walked over and started pouring punch for them. Clancy disappeared into the back room. I figured she'd reappear with a pot of coffee, as she usually did.

I tried to steer Sheila toward the back room. "Please. You're making a spectacle of yourself. You can't do this. Not in front of my guests."

"Really?" She turned to stare at my crafters. My hand was still on her arm, but she was doing her best to twist away. "Is that how you see it? I see it entirely differently. Actually I'm educating them. Showing them the *real* you. They think you're such a nice person. Miss Goody-Goody Two Shoes. But you're not. You're the person who's taking my grandkids away from me. The person who used me when she was down and out and didn't have a friend in the world. Back then, I could pick up your child every day of the week, couldn't I?"

To punctuate her claim, she yanked her arm out of my grasp. As she did, I caught a whiff of alcohol on her breath. The smoky scent of whiskey rolled off of her in waves.

"Sheila, that's enough! This is my store. I'm in the middle of teaching a class, and you need to leave, now."

"That's rich," she said. "Your store? You don't own anything but a bank note. Don't you dare try to make me leave. I can stay here as long as I like."

"No, you aren't. I'm here to take you home." The booming voice of Robbie Holmes rang out as he walked through the front door.

CHAPTER 50

I tried to recover my composure after Sheila's visit, but I couldn't. I did my best to smile and act like I wasn't upset, but inside I was quaking like a San Francisco earthquake.

Time in a Bottle had always been my sanctuary. Sure, we'd had our share of ugly situations. Once an estranged ex-husband beat up his wife in our back room. Another time we thwarted a misguided burglar. Yes, the list of bad moments could go on and on, but they paled in comparison to all the joy the store brought me and my friends on a daily basis.

The fact that Sheila had shown up here and dumped her dirty laundry for my guests to see really hurt. The pain went deep. If she had slapped me across the face, it wouldn't have been nearly as traumatic.

No one can hurt you like family can. Their words fly like heat-seeking missiles aimed at our hearts, and when they hit, which they inevitably do, they cause double the agony because we're the ones who gave them the live ammo. In the course of interacting with family, we provide them with a catalog of our hopes and dreams, our failures as well as our successes. They know full well what frightens us, and how to turn our fears into lethal weapons.

Sheila had been correct when she said that I owed her a lot. If it hadn't been for her, we couldn't have gotten Erik enrolled at CALA. He'd come to us late in the summer, long after enrollment for this school year had closed. I had petitioned the headmaster, Elliott McMahan requesting that he accept Erik, because he was soon to be Anya's brother.

"He should get accepted," I'd told Detweiler. "My friend, Maggie Earhart, told me that she has room in her kindergarten classroom for one more child. CALA is always trying to reach out to minorities because their ethnic mix is overwhelming white and Christian."

But a form letter came back to me saying that I'd missed the enrollment deadline. I called and made an appointment. The soonest I could have an "audience" was two weeks away.

"Sure," I had told Elliott's secretary. "If that's the best you can do, I'll take it."

I had dressed carefully for my meeting with Elliott McMahan. He's a pompous, stuffed trout who always looks past me at functions, as though I don't exist. On the day of my appointment, he stared at my burgeoning belly and practically sneered. "My, my, but your family is growing. While I congratulate you on your new son, unfortunately, this boy Aaron—"

"Erik."

"Erik is not a legacy. Therefore, we can't add

him to our roster. It's too late in the game."

"Late in the game?" I wasn't sure that I'd heard him right. "But school hasn't even started!"

"It has for us, Mrs. Lowenstein," Elliott said, in his most lofty tone. "I believe we're done here."

Despite all my efforts to muster up another argument, Elliott proceeded to shuffle papers around on his desk while he ignored me.

Finally, I had no choice but to leave his office. Our meeting had come on a particularly emotional day.

Getting a dose of snobbery from Elliott totally tipped me into despair. I didn't even make it to my car before I was wiping away tears. The security guard hustled over to ask if I was all right. After he escorted me to my car, I sat there in the driver's seat, wondering how on earth I'd cope with two kids in two different schools, and a new baby on the way. Even with Brawny's help, the logistics seemed overwhelming.

I came home from my meeting with Elliott with my tail tucked between my legs and my eyes red from crying. When Anya and I were alone, while Eric was engrossed in a video, she asked me how the meeting had gone. I told her.

"Are you upset?"

"Of course I am."

"I am, too. I want to be there for Erik, and I can't help him as much if we aren't in the same school. That's my job now, because I'm his big sister."

That almost set off another tidal wave of tears.

To top it all off, Detweiler text-messaged to say he'd be home late.

After dinner, I put both the kids to bed early. I thought I was safe, crying into my pillow, but Anya overheard me.

CHAPTER 51

The next day Anya told Sheila what had happened. My mother-in-law called me to ask if my daughter had her facts straight.

"Yup," I said.

"Did you just say, 'Yup'? For goodness sake, Kiki. No wonder they didn't let that child in. You talk like a Hoosier."

I was glad she couldn't see me thumb my nose at her. Only in Missouri (pronounced "misery" by some) did people use the term "Hoosier" as a pejorative. I mean, really?

"Believe me, Sheila, my white trash vocabulary had nothing to do with whether they admitted Erik or not. Elliott barely gave me the time of day. He told me the school roster was already set and sent me packing."

"Honestly, does it matter whether the boy goes to CALA?" she asked in that cool tone I knew so well.

"Yes, it does. First of all, if he has to go to some other school, that means he'll probably be on an entirely different schedule from Anya. We won't be able to take family vacations together.

Much less navigate snow days and teachers' institute. Second, it will make picking up and dropping off the kids a huge hassle. Last but not least, it really, really bothers Anya. As far as she's concerned, Erik is her brother. She knows how hard this transition has already been for him. Having him on the same campus is her way of taking responsibility for him—and frankly, I think her concern shows a lot of character on her part. She's growing up, Sheila. The school is standing in the way of her becoming a more thoughtful, mature young woman."

"That's your story," said Sheila.

I sighed. "Ask her yourself."

So she did.

"Of course, I want him to go to CALA," Anya told her grandmother. "You always say it's the best school in the state. That's why you wanted me to go here. Why shouldn't he go there, too? Besides, he's my brother. I want to look out for him."

When that didn't move her grandmother, Anya played her trump card. "I'm surprised you'd let Elliott bully Mom this way. After all, Erik's your grandson, too."

That did it. Anya knew her grandmother's well-shod Achilles heel.

"Well, well, well," Sheila had said, calling me later that day. "I guess that I shall have to pay Elliott a visit and see what we can do about getting Erik into CALA."

Like many alumnae, Sheila thought of the school as a sacred institution. She never missed a school board meeting. She had reserved seats at

every school function, including the famous May
Day ceremony. The employees who worked in the
admin office practically genuflected when Sheila
walked in. The development director called once a
week and offered to run little errands for her, like
picking up her dry-cleaning. This obsequious
behavior was not without merit. Sheila's will
includes a hefty bequest for the school.

Okay, the bequest isn't quite as showy as
footing the bill to add a new building to campus,
but it still has certain panache. In fact, the alum
director told me that a financial gift like Sheila's is
incredibly important to CALA.

"Mrs. Lowenstein hasn't tied it to any specific
project. That means that the headmaster is free to
use the money as he sees fit. Control of the funds
goes to Elliott," she explained. Lowering her
voice, the alum director added, "Elliott loves
being in the driver's seat."

The day after Elliott refused my request, Sheila
marched into the headmaster's office. Unlike me,
she hadn't called ahead for an appointment.

She didn't need one.

Instead, she sailed past Elliott's secretary and
took a seat in front of Elliott's desk.

"I want Erik Detweiler enrolled here at
CALA—and I want it done right now. Today.
Doesn't matter what his last name is. I don't care
that he missed early admission. He's my
granddaughter's brother and that makes him my
grandson."

"Come now, Sheila," said Elliott. "We've
already put together our class rosters. Besides, the
child isn't really a relative of yours. That would be

a genetic impossibility!"

Wrong move. Sarcasm is lost on Sheila.

She proceeded to give the headmaster a piece of her mind. In fact, she slammed him with her entire frontal lobe.

"You do realize, Elliott, that Erik is as good as adopted, don't you? Kiki is my daughter-in-law. She's carrying Detective Chad Detweiler's baby. They plan to get married, and I'll see that she does. That will make Chad Detweiler my son-in-law. Erik is Chad Detweiler's legal son. If you turn the boy down, what's the message you're sending to other adoptive parents in the CALA family?"

Then Elliott made a huge error in judgment. He said, "But Sheila, your real link to Kiki Lowenstein has now passed on. George has been dead, what? Nearly two years?"

"How dare you?" shouted Sheila.

("How dare you?" being Sheila's new favorite phrase.)

"Now, Sheila..." Elliott tried to be conciliatory, but the damage had already been done.

"Don't you *dare* evoke the name of my dead son! We're talking about a minority student here, Elliott. Do you really want CALA to be known as the school that turned down a child because he was bi-racial? Especially a boy? I ask you to consider this carefully, because that's how I'll spin this. I'll go directly to the media and tell them that you rejected Erik because his birth father was African-American," and she paused long enough to smile before adding, "Imagine what angry crowds could do to the grounds of CALA. Think of the damage to all those flowers your wife plants so carefully every year."

The old "think of your flowers" routine. I'd have to remember that one!

Elliott looked as if he might hurl his lunch.

For good measure, Sheila lobbed her last hand grenade at him. "Furthermore, if you don't accept the boy right this minute, you'll never see a penny of my money when I'm gone."

Elliott caved.

Later I learned that Sheila stood over the man while he typed up Erik's admittance letter.

How do I know all of this?

While my mother-in-law talked to Elliott, Anya sat outside of his office where she could overhear every word.

Yes, my daughter got a real education that day. She learned the power of a name, the importance of belonging, and how leverage, when properly applied, could move an intractable object. Sheila had shown my daughter her commitment to us as a family.

I really did owe Sheila a lot.

But that didn't mean she had the right to show up at my store and make ugly scenes in front of my customers.

CHAPTER 52

Even though it was nearly ten when I got home, Erik and Anya were wide awake. Erik couldn't wait to show me the picture of him sitting on Santa's lap.

"Mama Kiki, I was brave!" he said, emphasizing that last word.

"I can see that you were."

"The Detweilers left about an hour ago," said Brawny. "They needed to get back so they could be up bright and early to make it to their granddaughter Emily's holiday pageant at school tomorrow morning."

"I wish I hadn't missed them." Leaning over, I planted a kiss on Anya's cheek. "Sounds like Erik had a good time. How about you?"

Her smile was incredibly grown-up. "It was cool to be there with him."

We spent thirty minutes rehashing their visit with the Detweilers, before I put them both to bed. By then, I was exhausted. My feet had swollen to twice their usual size.

I wanted desperately to talk to Detweiler, but he'd text-messaged to say that he was working late to try and get caught up on reports so he could enjoy himself on Christmas Eve and Christmas.

Since we'd met, I'd learned that paperwork was a perennial pain in his backside, the part of his job that never ended, even after a creep was sentenced to prison.

After a long hot shower, I crawled under the covers. That's when I realized that I had totally forgotten to return Eudora's Zentangle supplies to Ester. The events of the day started to tumble through my head, like a flip chart stocked with "This Is Your Life" scenes.

I should have felt snug and secure. My new diamond reminded me that I was loved. The covers were pulled up to my chin. My bed smelled faintly of lavender, an attempt by Brawny to help me get more sleep. Tonight, however, it wasn't working. My mind was racing and my baby was auditioning for the Rockettes. I guess he knew his mama was upset.

Because I was.

I was angry, tired, and lonely.

But not hungry because the minute I'd climbed into my car, I'd started stuffing my mouth with leftover monkey bread and shortbread cookies. By the time I pulled into our driveway, I was sick from eating so many sweets. Overeating is not a coping strategy that I recommend. Recognizing what I had done, I asked myself, "Am I really any better than Sheila? I'm acting like an addict, too!"

At least my little excursions into stuffing down feelings were done in private. As a matter of fact, I rarely overeat in front of other people. It is only when I can sneak away that I'd use food as my drug of choice. As a child of a pair of alcoholics, my particular weakness is sugar. The more I eat of it, the more I crave.

I wondered if all addicts rationalized their behavior. If we all hated ourselves after we'd indulged. Maybe Sheila was lying awake in her bed and feeling horrible about what she'd done, too.

That left me staring at our ceiling, thinking about our encounter.

It was far too reminiscent of growing up in an alcoholic home.

She'd pushed every one of those buttons that I'd worked for years to hide.

And of course, she'd totally embarrassed me in front of my customers. People who paid to have a relaxing evening away from their own dramas.

Instead, they'd gotten a front row seat at mine!

Although Laurel and Clancy had assured me that our crafters weren't upset, I was. Thank goodness Clancy had the foresight to text-message Robbie Holmes so quickly. Otherwise, how would I have dealt with a raging Sheila?

The thought came to me: If it had been anyone else, I would have called the police and had the drunk dragged out of the store.

Okay.

So was I willing to do that to Sheila?

And if I didn't, did that make me an enabler?

CHAPTER 53

Thursday, December 15...

I woke up to rumpled sheets and a cold bed.

Detweiler had come home, slipped in beside me, and gotten up before I'd opened my eyes. Throwing on clothes, I padded downstairs, hoping to catch him before he left for work.

"There's the girl I love," he said, as I threw myself into his arms. Fortunately, he'd already drained his coffee cup, or he'd have poured it down my back. The strength of his arms made me feel totally secure, and for the first time since Sheila's unwelcome visit to my store, I felt myself relax.

In a babble of disconnected phrases and unintelligible sentences, I told him about Sheila's drunken tirade.

"So that's where Robbie raced off to," said Detweiler. "We were discussing an upcoming court appearance when he looked down at his phone. Next thing I know, I'm standing there alone. He must have put on the lights and sirens to make it to your store so fast."

"And that's not all," I said, eager to tell him

about Detective Vasquez.

"Slow down, babe. Sit down and have some scrambled eggs, and then we can talk. Brawny left some in the oven on warm, before she went out for her run. There's a rack of toast in there, too. Hot tea in the pot under the cozy."

I poured myself a cup. "She thinks of everything."

He grinned. "I have to admit, she's the best labor saving device I've ever come across."

After sliding a plate my way, he said, "Eat some eggs while they're hot. Now, what else happened yesterday?"

I told him about Detective Vasquez's appearance.

"Interesting." Detweiler crossed those long legs of his. "He's a good cop. Of course, he didn't tell you whether they changed their minds and decided that Eudora Field's death was a homicide, did he?"

"No, but I pointed out to him that since the attending physician says she died of a heart attack, he has no 'means' to work with. That's what Caitlyn told us. She texted us after her grandmother got word to her about Eudora's passing. There's no reason for Caitlyn to be lying, is there?"

"My sweet little sleuth." He leaned over to kiss me. "You've been involved in entirely too many crimes."

"Believe me, it's a hobby I want to walk away from. By the way, you wouldn't happen to know if Vasquez is married, would you?"

Detweiler raised an eyebrow at me. "Yes, I

would know. But I'm not sure that I care to share."

"Not for me, silly." I gave him a playful shove. "For Clancy."

"He's a widower. His wife died of ovarian cancer six years ago."

"How sad." Secretly I was a little relieved. Clancy is rarely interested in the men who happen her way. She's incredibly finicky, in a lovely, old-fashioned type of way. "Just so you know, I'll probably need to talk to Detective Vasquez again."

"Why?" Detweiler got up and poured himself another cup of coffee. I loved watching the muscles across his shoulders move. He was one gorgeous man, and I was very lucky that for whatever reason he'd fallen in love with me!

I explained what I'd learned about Cecily Kelly's husband, Peter, and how Eudora had killed off his rose bushes. "Then there's Marvela's daughter, Beth. She was hoping to get a volleyball scholarship, but Eudora forced her to take a test early and she flunked it. That caused Beth to lose her spot on the team, and her scholarship hopes went down the drain. I saved the best for last. Ester would have been out on the streets if Eudora hadn't given her a place to live. While they shared a house, Eudora made her sister's life miserable."

Detweiler pursed his lips into a low whistle. "Sure sounds to me like a lot of people had valid reasons to want Eudora Field dead."

CHAPTER 54

On my way from the parking lot into the store, I noticed that same slick spot of ice where I'd fallen. The hazard ticked me off, because I'd personally salted and sprinkled sand over the area twice the day before. But as I looked more carefully—and as Gracie nearly lost her footing—I recognized the underlying problem. There was a tiny dip in the asphalt. The pavement had formed a shallow bowl deep enough for water to collect. Even if we salted and sanded the parking lot again, that particular spot would continue to be treacherous. Fixing it would have to wait until spring.

I took Gracie inside, put her in her crate, and went out to move my car so that my passenger side door was almost on top of the spot. Sure, someone could take the slot to my right, but they'd have to encroach on my space to do so. Since I knew about the danger, and since Gracie could hop in on the driver's side, I was preventing a customer from taking a pratfall as I had.

Being the first person to arrive at my store always gives me a thrill. There are mornings when I pinch myself, thinking back to the day when Dodie hired me, and reflecting on how far I've come. They say that pride goeth before a fall. I sincerely hoped that's not true because I am incredibly proud of the changes I've made. Dodie might not agree with them, but they are working well for our customers.

For example, I had casters added to all the shelf units on our central sales floor. That allows us to scrunch the shelves together to create an improvised open area for our classes and crops.

I have turned the unused portion of our back room into a dedicated space for other crafts, mainly needle arts. A small table has been added so that knitters and crocheters can pull up chairs and work on their projects.

Over time I have installed more security features like mirrors and panic buttons. These buttons are tucked away in hidden places, like under my work table, where they can be easily accessed in case of an emergency. One push and an alarm is triggered that should bring the local police running.

Moving around the store, I straightened shelves and returned merchandise to their rightful spots. This sort of tidying up usually takes place after our last evening session. But immediately following the icosahedron class with the Crafty Cuties, I'd taught a class with enrollment open to the public. That meant catering to the needs of thirty-eight eager students, enough people to keep Clancy, Laurel, and me hopping until we locked the front door at quarter till nine. The eager customers left us exhausted. I thanked my co-workers for their extraordinary efforts and suggested that we all call it a night. I promised to show up bright and early this morning to get the store ready for another day. And here I was, doing exactly that. Glancing overhead, I noticed that most of the Christmas stockings showed highlighter ink. That meant that most of them had been used to fulfill a customer's wish list.

Hot dog! I did a little dance jig of happiness.

The back door opened and shut. I wrinkled my nose at the appetizing smell of gingerbread. Margit was teaching a gingerbread man decorating class tonight. It had been billed as a "family friendly" session. Brawny would pick up Erik and Anya, swing by the store, drop them off, and take Gracie back home with her. That would give me the chance to enjoy this special class with my children. Although the students would be crafting their ornaments out of polymer clay, Margit had baked real gingerbread muffins for them to munch while the clay baked in the oven.

A little kick in my belly reminded me that soon my time would be divided three ways. I sent up a prayer that I could make all three of my children feel loved and special. For good measure, I asked God to look after Sheila.

"I think she's too proud to ask you herself," I whispered. "But we both know she needs you. Something's going on in her head. A pain that she's trying to ease with the booze. Please help her, God."

To give my prayer a little extra power, I dug around under the counter. As a holiday gift, a customer had given me a tiny white candle in a cute decorative holder. I lit it.

A sense of peace flowed through me.

For right now—and that was all I had, this moment—all was well in my world.

CHAPTER 55

Friday, December 16...

When I woke up on Friday, the winter landscape was a monochromatic scene in shades of dull gray, broken up by contrasting swathes of deep, dark evergreen. A slow brightening of the world revealed these to be blue-green pines and fresh green rickrack shapes of holly, enlivened by the true red of the berries. Slowly a dusting of snow performed a magic trick, transforming the back yard into a fantastical wonderland, complete with sparkling sequins.

Cara Mia's flight would be arriving at one, so I volunteered to take the kids to school while Brawny tidied up our guest room.

Erik had proudly wrapped his polymer clay gingerbread man in red tissue paper with the intention of giving it to Miss Maggie. To keep his project from getting broken, I'd taped the ornament onto a piece of sturdy cardboard that Eric had decorated with vivid markers.

Anya stood there watching me. "I wonder if Erik knows how lucky he is to have a crafty mother."

The unexpected compliment caused a lump in my throat. "That's very sweet of you."

"Honestly," she said, "I can't count the times your craft supplies have bailed me out of a jam with my school work. The other kids had crummy letters falling off their projects, but not me. Remember that time I had the labels wrong? Mr. Penderson came up and told me? That man was such a meanie. He wasn't much of a teacher and loved catching people making mistakes. When he saw what I'd done, he laughed and said, 'Too late to fix it,' but you'd shown me how to use Velcro dots. So I took down the labels and switched them. When he came back with the judging committee, he said, 'It's too bad that this student labeled her steps wrong, because otherwise this is A-plus work.' Then one of the other teachers pointed out that everything was labelled correctly. Penderson's mouth dropped open, he turned and stared at me. I wanted to yell, 'Psych!' But I didn't."

"I remember him. He's the guy who wouldn't help you when you asked questions about the process. I guess he didn't understand he was supposed to actually be teaching you, not just grading your papers and tests."

"That reminds me," she said, picking up her own backpack. "You'll never guess who's playing Mary in the Nativity play."

"What Nativity play?"

"The one that church down the street is putting on. The people who are borrowing Monroe. Remember? Brawny asked, and you said it was okay." I put the gingerbread man into a gift bag. Erik had labored over each detail, much to my delight. Margit had been so kind to him, encouraging his creativity. My friend Maggie was going to love this gift!

"The Nativity play? Church down the street? Oh, right! I give up. Who's playing Mary?"

"Brittany Ladarov."

"You are kidding me?" I remembered Brittany, because every mother remembers the first kid who picks on her child. Brittany was a bully back in first grade, and from what I'd heard, her talents for making other children miserable had only grown more refined over the years.

"Nope. Cross my heart."

"How'd you find that out?"

"She's best friends with Lisa Stemphill."

"Terrific," I said, sarcastically. "That's what they call casting against type. From all I've been taught, Mary was meek and mild, a good person through and through."

"Yeah," said Anya. "I'll never forget when she told me my father was going to hell because he wasn't Christian."

"I remember. That was right after George died. She sought you out at a soccer game. Hadn't seen you in years, but she came over especially to deliver that message of solace. What a little witch!"

Reaching over, I pulled my daughter close. "That still hurts, doesn't it, baby?"

"It sure does," she said, in a husky voice.

"Brittany was awfully concerned about your dad, but she should have been worrying about her own salvation. The Jews are God's Chosen People. Besides, Brittany isn't a Christian either. Not really. She can't show me one single place in the Bible where Jesus Christ was purposefully hurtful. Over and over again, he treated other people with love, understanding, and compassion. That's why we celebrate his birth. Now does that sound like Brittany to you?"

"Not hardly," said Anya.

CHAPTER 56

Once again, I parked next to the slick spot, hoping to keep my customers from sliding on that nasty place like I had. This morning, Margit had gotten into the store before I did. Clancy arrived soon after. Her arms were loaded down with baskets we'd be using for the spa items the next day. I helped her unburden herself.

"Fair warning, ladies. At twelve-thirty, I'm heading to the airport to pick up Cara Mia," I said. "We plan to have lunch together. I should be back to the store around two-thirty. Three at the latest."

"Laurel is coming in early to help with customers and to prep for her snowman luminaria class. I'm going to gather up all my supplies," said Clancy. "How'd the gingerbread man class go last night?"

I used my phone to show her the photos. In most of them, Margit posed side-by-side with my son. The last picture was of a very proud Erik showing off his finished gingerbread man. As the older woman passed by, I tilted my phone so she could see the images, too. "Margit, I think Erik's in love with you."

"*Ja.* He has won my heart. Such a good little boy. That reminds me. There was a message for you on the phone this morning. A detective? I wrote down his name and number."

I stepped into my office and picked up the pink "While You Were Out" pad. Margit was incredibly precise about copying down all the information we needed to return calls. There in her schoolgirl handwriting was Detective Vasquez's personal cell phone number and the fact that he intended to either drop by or call me back later during the day.

Clancy turned bright eyes on me. "So?"

"He might stop by." I explained what I'd learned about motives that the other Crafty Cuties might have for wanting Eudora dead.

"You don't really think that any of those sweet little crafters would have killed Eudora Field, do you?" Clancy lifted a perfectly shaped eyebrow at me.

"Nah, not really. But I'm worried that I inadvertently pointed the finger at Caitlyn and Lois Singer by explaining why they had reason to be angry with Eudora. And as you heard, Brad Oxemann told them that Laurel has a motive. Even though you did a great job of discounting that notion."

"So your goal is to further muddy the waters," said Clancy.

"I guess." I paused. "After all, they don't have a means. Eudora died of natural causes."

"I wouldn't be so sure of that." Clancy shook her head. "I bumped into Chloe Chang at the gas station on my way home from work yesterday.

Did you know her husband is a heart surgeon?"

"Yes. So what?"

"I asked her if a person could die of a broken heart. She told me that they absolutely can. Then I specifically asked her if you could give someone a heart attack."

"And she said?"

"Positively without question. There are documented cases of people getting scared or overly excited and dropping dead."

"So it isn't an old wives' tale?" I couldn't believe what I was hearing.

"No, that's why they have those signs up at amusement parks advising people with heart problems not to ride the roller coasters. It's especially dangerous if the person has an underlying heart condition. In fact, there's some evidence that ongoing angina attacks can weaken the heart, even if the patient is being treated for them with nitro. The theory is that the angina can wear down the heart muscle over time."

"*Ja,* I know this is true," Margit joined us. "A woman in the care facility with my mother was frightened by a movie she saw. That night, the resident in the unit above hers dropped a book on the floor. An accident! That's all it was, but this woman, she died! Her heart! It quit because the noise had scared her so much."

If this was true—and I had to believe my friends were being forthright—then someone might have murdered Eudora Field. And the crime could have been committed right before my eyes!

"I looked it up when I got home," said Clancy. "We all have a basic 'fright or flight' reaction that produces a surge of catecholamines, a process known as sympathetic swamping. It can cause the heart to spasm or not squeeze as it should. Either response can be incompatible with life."

"Incompatible with life? What a fancy way to say a person can die!" Margit threw up her hands.

"That's fascinating," I told my friends. "Like it says in the Bible, we are 'fearfully and artfully made.'"

"Amen to that," said Clancy.

CHAPTER 57

Right at twelve-thirty, I hopped in my car and drove to Lambert International Airport. Cara Mia had messaged me to say she was carrying her bag. We agreed that I'd swing through the passenger pick-up lane rather than park my car.

Sure enough, I spotted her instantly. Unlike the other people who were bundled up, she wore a sweater and a light jacket. I think she'd forgotten how bone-chilling our cold weather could be.

"Hop in!" I called through the open passenger side window. "You must be freezing."

"I sure am. All my heavy winter clothes are still up here in storage."

"Then let's run by your storage locker first," I said, as I pulled forward out of the angled spaces and into the flow of departing vehicles.

That detour took us half an hour, but it proved to be time well-spent. Cara quickly found the wardrobe box containing her winter coat, hats, and gloves. "I had a scarf," she said, shaking her head, "but I can't remember where I put it."

"Let's go eat lunch at Bread Co.," I suggested, calling the chain by the name all St. Louis residents know, and making sure that "Co." rhymes with "dough."

"Fantastic."

I noticed she'd gotten a touch of sun. The color in her face complimented her dark curls. "We have Panera Bread down in Florida, but that doesn't seem the same as eating at Bread Co. I know it's just another name for the same chain of cafes, but somehow I can't get used to it."

As I drove, she told me about her new store, The Treasure Chest. In particular, I was happy to hear that she'd made two wonderful friends, MJ Austin, an older woman familiar with vintage Florida goods, and Skye Blue, a young crafter who was also Cara's new tenant.

"How's your apartment upstairs over the shop coming? Have you decorated it yet? Dish, girlfriend!"

Cara had a sure eye for color and texture. She'd done several thrifty makeovers for our mutual friends, as well as renovating her family restaurant. Her house, the one in which she raised her son, was a treat to visit. The place looked like a model home in the HGTV Magazine.

"No," she said with a certain hesitation, "and I can't tell you why. Sure, I'm busy, but I was busy when I ran the restaurant. It's like there's something holding me back. I can't explain it, but I don't really belong in that apartment."

"The good news is that you don't have to think about it. Not today or tomorrow. You're here now, so just enjoy yourself. I want to hear all about your recycled and upcycled merchandise."

Over soup and sandwiches, she went on and

on, detailing one project after another. I was amazed at how she'd managed to stock her store so fast. "Florida is full of thrift shops. Skye, MJ, and I can spot raw talent. We buy things that are old, ugly, and worn. Then we transform them into objects of desire."

I'd never seen Cara so happy, and I started to tell her so, when my cell phone rang. It was Clancy. "I hate to interrupt you while you're having lunch with Cara Mia, but we have a problem. A big problem."

"What's up?"

"The supplies for my spa baskets didn't come in. We've turned this place upside down, and they aren't here. Margit is going through her inventory sheets for the second time, but so far, it looks like the things were never shipped. Kiki, we have twenty-five people signed up for this project! They'll be here early tomorrow for the class. What am I going to do?"

"I'll be right there," I said. "We're finishing our food. Don't panic, Clancy. We'll figure something out."

I'd no more than ended my call when my phone rang again. This time it was Detective Vasquez. "Mrs. Lowenstein? We need to talk."

CHAPTER 58

"I thought you were going to quit playing amateur detective," said Cara Mia Delgatto, as we climbed into my car after I hung up from talking with Raoul Vasquez.

"You'd think, wouldn't you?" I said, casting a rueful glance at my belly. Since there wasn't a lot of traffic on Old Olive, I could do that. But as we got closer to 40, I had to keep my eyes on the road.

Cara laughed. "I could have used your help when I tripped over that dead body in my store."

"You did perfectly fine without me. As for me giving up on snooping around, all I can say is, it's not my fault! I was minding my own business, teaching a Zentangle class—"

"You're telling me that you were teaching a class designed to help people live longer, happier, stress-free lives, and someone died?" Cara started laughing so hard that tears rolled down her cheeks.

"I hadn't even started teaching that particular class when this woman grabbed her chest and fell off her scooter!"

Cara stopped long enough to echo, "Her scooter? This was a group of senior citizens?"

As I turned toward the store, I explained my relationship with the Crafty Cuties. I also walked Cara through a chronological account of the events after Eudora had been taken to the hospital.

"Wait! Is that Eudora Field, the Spanish teacher?"

"Right. Laurel had her for Latin at Viz, but I guess Eudora taught Spanish as well."

"I'm older than Laurel, so I had Miss Field before she decided she wanted to be a nun. She taught Spanish at my parochial school. After she taught at Viz, she came back and taught Spanish part-time. Headed up the Spanish club."

"From everything I've heard, she was a mean teacher." I told Cara about Laurel's uniform violations and Beth Castillo being forced to take a mid-term she wasn't ready for. "In fact, all the Crafty Cuties had reasons to be angry with Eudora. All except for Ruby LeCuero."

"She has the best reason of all," said Cara.

"What do you mean?" We joined a line of cars exiting at Brentwood. A signal chimed on my dashboard to alert me that the surface temperature of the roads had dropped below freezing. I took extra care to allow a car length or two between me and my fellow motorists.

"You didn't hear about Ruby's husband? Hector? He worked as a janitor at one of the other Catholic schools. St. Joan's, maybe? Or St. Cecilia's? Anyway, Miss Field accused him of breaking into her car and stealing her purse. She'd parked outside for a language club meeting.

Hector was fired on the spot because it was Miss Field's word against his. He didn't have his citizenship papers yet, so he had to go back to Mexico. Bringing him here again was a costly process. I guess once you've messed up with immigration, it's harder to gain entry. Actually, I'm surprised that Ruby would be part of any club that included Eudora Field. Especially given that Miss Field practically ruined the LeCueros' lives."

CHAPTER 59

Clancy hurried out to greet us as I pulled into the lot. "What on earth am I going to do about the missing soaps? We've promoted this class as the chance to put together a sumptuous grouping of handmade spa products to give as a gift or keep for yourself! Instead, I've got empty baskets and shredded colored paper!"

"Calm down," I told her. Since she's only been teaching a short while, she is the least resilient of my merry maids. I suspect that Clancy has a slight touch of OCD. It flares up when she's under stress. Panic showed in the whites of her eyes, but before I could calm her down, a black Escalade pulled into the lot and out stepped Detective Vasquez.

Emotions fought to take over Clancy's face. Panic, joy, surprise, fear, and then an attack of nerves.

Cara Mia glanced at the big black car and then turned her attention to Clancy. "I can help you. I've had a lot of experience with spa products. Let's go inside and see what you have already. Then we can figure out what to do."

"B-b-but..." Clancy couldn't take her eyes off of Vasquez. As he walked toward us, the slightest smile played around his lips, a sure sign that he shared her interest.

"Go on," I told her. "I'll bring him inside. Once you and Cara get this sorted, you'll have the chance to chat with him."

"About what?"

Vasquez had turned around and gone back to his car, obviously having forgotten something. That gave Clancy the chance to be flustered a little longer.

"You could invite him to something," I said quickly.

Cara noticed the obvious attraction between the two and added, "Great idea! After all, it's Christmas! Tell you what, Clancy, why don't you invite him to the holiday party tomorrow night at my restaurant? You two can come as my guests."

"Y-y-your place?" Her eyes were huge.

I'd never seen Clancy like this. Cupid's arrow must have been soaked in Love Potion Number Nine, because she was totally turning to mush over this guy.

"Remember? Her family restaurant. It's called Cara Mia's." I reached over, grabbed Clancy's shoulders and gave her a little shake. "Over on The Hill. Two blocks off of Gravois."

"This is really simple," said Cara. "All you need to do is tell the nice detective that you've been invited, and it seems like a waste to go alone when there's going to be great food and super wine."

"What if he's married?" This question was

Clancy's last ditch effort. Her indecision kept her frozen to the icy pavement. A light snow had started to fall. The flakes were big as quarters.

"He's not," I said. "I asked Detweiler."

Right then, the handsome homicide detective strolled over to my car. "Ladies? Do you mind if I borrow Mrs. Lowenstein? I promise to bring her right back."

"Only if you walk her into the store when you're done," said Clancy. She'd obviously regained her composure. "Kiki slipped and fell out here the other day. We don't want it happening again."

"Of course not," said Detective Vasquez. "I promise I'll walk her inside and deliver her to you, Mrs. Whitehead, personally."

"Clancy," she said. "Remember?"

"And I'm Raoul," he said, to her and her alone.

I fought the urge to smile. Cara Mia kept a straight face, but her eyes twinkled

Clancy and Raoul stared at each other, with looks so steamy that the ice started to melt from under our feet.

"Good," said Clancy, with a toss of her head. "I'll look forward to seeing you later."

Way to go, girlfriend!

CHAPTER 60

With a courtly flourish, Detective Vasquez took my arm and walked me to his car, the unmarked Escalade that sure didn't look like a police cruiser. After opening the door, he waited until I was seated, and then he closed the door carefully. A layer of snow, as fluffy as egg whites, slid down my window and disappeared.

Even before he climbed in, the interior smelled of his spicy cologne. I picked out a musky undertone and a hint of sage. Very Southwestern.

"Nice car," I said, enjoying the masculine fragrance.

"It's good for blending in. Do you like coffee?"

"I adore it, but I can only drink decaf right now."

"How does a trip to Kaldi's sound?" His smile was kind.

"Perfect." I loved the local chain. They were the ones who taught me the legend about the goat herder who "discovered" coffee. He noticed that his animals were much more active and alert after eating beans from a nearby shrub.

After carefully pulling onto Brentwood,

Vasquez asked, "At the risk of being inappropriate, when is your baby due?"

"January fifteenth. You're fine. I'm not trying to pretend that I'm not pregnant. In fact, I recently got formally engaged. See?"

He glanced over. "Good for you and for Detweiler. Like I said before, he's a keeper."

At Kaldi's, he was every bit as solicitous, taking my arm so I wouldn't fall. Fortunately, they'd already salted and sanded their walks, because the snow was beginning to stick. After ordering a decaf latte for me, and encouraging me to choose an iced reindeer cookie, he filled his own cup with black coffee and guided me to a booth.

"You said you have new information for me."

I settled in and told him what I'd learned about all the members of the Crafty Cuties. "Taking it from the top, Suspect #1 is Ester Field Robinson. Ester was Eudora's sister. When their parents died, they left the house to Eudora because they thought that Ester was happily married, but the Ester's husband took off left her penniless. Ester was forced to move in with Eudora, who made her life miserable. The two were always arguing, but without Eudora's help, Ester would have been out on the streets. Now that Eudora is dead, the house belongs to Ester.

"Suspect #2 is Caitlyn Robinson, Ester's granddaughter and Eudora's great-niece. Eudora purposely broke Caitlyn's Demski award winning entry. That has jeopardized Caitlyn's chance for a scholarship to Indiana University. We won't know until January whether Caitlyn might be able to substitute a new piece of work and retain her right to the scholarship. So far, it doesn't look promising.

"Suspect #3 is Lois Singer. Eudora put out poisoned meat to kill Lois's cat, Tabby, because he kept pooping in Eudora's yard.

"Suspect #4 is Marvela Castillo. Her daughter, Beth, got a low grade in Latin because Eudora made her take a mid-term as soon as she returned to school after being out with the flu. The low grade cost Beth her spot on the girls' volleyball team.

"Suspect #5 is Ruby LeCuero. Eudora got Ruby's husband, Hector, fired from his job as a janitor. Got him deported, too.

"Suspect #6 is Cecily Kelly. Because Eudora was jealous of Cecily's husband Peter's rose bed, she sprayed the flowers with Round Up and killed everything."

He dutifully wrote all this down. "How about Laurel Wilkins? Do you think I can safely cross her off the list?"

Rather than launch into a defense of Laurel, I tried to stay objective. "You heard what Clancy said about Laurel having to take the SAT over. Doesn't sound like much of a reason to me. Laurel has been very successful in college, so I can't see that Eudora did her any harm, can you?"

"How about you? Brad Oxemann has told me that you love being the center of a murder investigation. That you'll do anything for the chance to prove you're our city's own Miss Marple and Jessica Fletcher rolled into one. What do you say about that?" Vasquez never raised his voice or changed his tone even though his words were inflammatory.

"I say 'bunk.' It would be pretty tough to keep a business running if I killed all my customers one by one. While Eudora wasn't my favorite person on earth, I had no reason to want to see her dead."

He nodded. "Want a refill?"

"No thanks." I waited as he topped off his cup of coffee. When he sat back down, I said, "You must have reason to believe that Eudora's death wasn't of natural causes."

He said nothing.

"Clancy found out that people can die of fright. That a good scare or ongoing stress can cause a heart attack, especially if the person already has a weak heart. Is that what happened with Eudora?"

Vasquez lifted chocolate brown eyes to me. "Why? Can you think of something that would have scared the victim? Did anything happen that would frighten her?"

"I didn't see anything frightening," I admitted. I thought about that a second. "Eudora did tell me that she was terribly afraid of spiders. A real case of arachnophobia."

"People with a history of heart problems and severe phobias usually carry nitroglycerin with them. Usually on their person."

"And she didn't have any?"

His smile was gentle. "I need to get you back to your store. You've been very helpful, Mrs. Lowenstein."

CHAPTER 61

I dreaded going back to Time in a Bottle. Although Cara Mia had volunteered to help Clancy, I wasn't sure what she could do about the missing spa supplies. Mentally, I kicked myself for leaving my friends with such a big problem to solve.

As soon as Detective Vasquez parked his car, I popped open my door. I'd stayed away long enough. Time to see what sort of crises that were brewing.

"Wait for me, please," he said, in that same unhurried voice he'd used throughout our interview.

Snow had started to stick. It covered the earth as sweetly as a mother tucks a blanket around a sleeping child.

Vasquez helped me step down onto the running board that automatically popped out whenever the car door opened.

As we moved toward the store, I asked him about his plans for Christmas.

"Since my wife Maritsa died, I don't do much. Funny how life works. I thought for sure I'd have a houseful of kids by now. It wasn't like we didn't try! Maritsa had female problems from the beginning. We went from one specialist to another. They say it's not true, but I think the hormones she was taking to get pregnant were the triggers for her cancer."

We paused at the back door. The snow was really piling up. I'd have to send someone outside with a shovel at this rate. "I am so sorry. Isn't life strange? I've gotten pregnant twice. Each time it seemed like the worst fate that could befall me. But looking back, I was blessed, wasn't I?"

"I think so. Life is rarely convenient. That's the ongoing question we all face. How will I deal with this change of plans? How do I create a joyful life while taking one detour after another? That is the true test of character. We can whine about our helplessness or we can move on."

"Are you moving on?"

"Christmas Eve I go to the mass at St. Toby's," he started, but I interrupted with, "That's right down the street from our house in Webster Groves!"

"Really? On Christmas Day, I have a ritual. I drink mulled cider and watch sappy holiday flicks until I get called into work. Since so many of the others have families, I sign up for holiday duty. That lets them stay home."

My hand was on the door knob, but I didn't turn it yet. "I think you should try something new this year."

"Really? What?"

I invited him to our house. "We can all go together to see the Christmas pageant. Our donkey is going to be part of the manger scene at St. Toby's."

"Your what?" His eyes lit up with amusement.

"Our donkey. Actually he belongs to our neighbor, but anyway, we'll have a huge feast right after. On Christmas Day, the house will be full with friends and family. Why don't you join us, at least for an hour or so? We'll eat at two in the afternoon."

Of course he hesitated. I could see him weighing the pros and cons. A snowflake landed on his lashes. The contrast of its whiteness against the deep brown of his eyes was startling.

I tossed him the clincher. "Clancy's coming."

He fought a smile, but the smile won. "All right. Sounds like a plan."

CHAPTER 62

"It looks like you brought Kiki back to us in one piece." Clancy nodded at Detective Raoul Vasquez with approval.

Gracie yodeled with happiness at the merry sound of our voices.

"Before I forget," said the detective, reaching inside his coat, "I picked up a bag of Kaldi's best roast for all of you. My way of saying 'thanks' for the coffee."

Although his words were directed to all of us, he looked at Clancy as he offered up the bag.

"Thank you," she said, rather primly.

The back room fairly crackled with mutual attraction. Cara suddenly feigned interest in the hem of her jeans, while Margit erased the same spot on her paperwork over and over. Only Gracie watched the two lovebirds with unabashed interest.

As I unwound my scarf, I said, "I need to go up front and check on the number of people signed up for tonight's class."

Cara Mia caught my drift. "Margit? Will you come with us?"

"*Neine,* I have work—" she started to protest, but I reached down and grabbed her by the arm.

"We really need your help," I said, hauling her to her feet.

She gave me a petulant stare. Then it dawned on her. "*Ja, ja,* I must show you who is signed up," Margit said with a wink.

The three of us—Margit, Cara, and I—left Clancy and Detective Vasquez alone in the back room.

On the sales floor, Cara showed us how she'd proposed we cope with the lack of the specialty supplies. "You had these plain white lunch sacks in the back, and a stock of plastic baggies. Clancy and I ran out and bought fragrance, food coloring, Epsom Salts, and sea salt. We'll mix up bath crystals, put them in the bags, and add labels. The bath salts will be every bit as cute as the other items would have been."

"Thank goodness," I said, happily. "Poor Clancy goes into a tailspin when there's a hitch in her plans."

"She did a pretty good job of staying calm. I reminded her that her computer is a valuable resource. We googled bath salts in nothing flat. Then we hopped over to Etsy to look at spa baskets and a variety of similar products. Did the same on Pinterest too. That gave us a lot of great ideas to work with. Clancy showed me two boxes of vanilla votive candles you had in storage. You've also got those small glass jars that the votives fit inside. Covering the jars and labeling them will go a long way toward making them look extra special."

Margit had moved over to the cash wrap station. Waving a clipboard, she said, "We have twenty-two people registered."

"And supplies for twenty-four," said Cara. "Margit, let's go sit in the needle arts room. We can kit up the materials in there."

Margit's gray head and Cara's dark curls bobbed along in an animated conversation as they walked toward the back of the store.

Cara's confidence had grown since she moved away from St. Louis. Although she'd encountered her share of challenges in Florida, she'd come to realize she was more creative and self-reliant than she'd thought. As long as she stayed here in St. Louis, she'd be known as the daughter of Thomas and Jolene Delgatto, and she would have forever compared herself to them and their successes. But the move to the Sunshine State had forced her to step out of the long shadows cast by her late parents. Truly, she'd blossomed in the sun.

I smiled to myself, feeling happy for my friend, when in stomped Brad Oxemann.

CHAPTER 63

"I know you did it," said Brad Oxemann. "I'm here to turn you in. I found the pictures of spiders! It's proof that you killed Eudora Field."

"What are you talking about?" I instinctively shrank away from his hulking form.

"See? I took these out of the trash. You made doodles of spiders." He waved discarded worksheets from our class.

"Those are standard patterns. I share them whenever I teach."

"I don't care how you try to spin it. You drew all these pictures of spiders. I happen to know that Miss Field was terrified of spiders. This is how you killed her, isn't it? You showed her these, and they terrified her. She would have used her nitroglycerin, but you swiped it from her, didn't you?"

With a lunge, he was on me. His free hand captured my elbow. He dug the tips of his fingers into the sensitive spot immediately above my funny bone. I couldn't believe how much it hurt. The world turned green before my eyes.

"I'm taking you in," said Brad, dragging me

toward the front door. "I'm closing the case."

Twisting away, I managed to loosen his painful grip and scream. "Let go of me!"

Any minute, Detective Vasquez would hear the ruckus and come to my rescue. All I needed was to stall, so I planted my feet and refused to follow Brad. He hadn't expected my resistance. Moving his fingers back to the sensitive spot, he reapplied pressure, causing me to wince. I panted with pain, trying to stay focused. Then a movement caught my attention.

Margit stepped quietly out of the needle arts room and darted over to the cash station.

What if Brad saw her?

I had to signal her to stay away. She froze at the counter. Her eyes were huge behind those almond-shaped glasses.

I twisted against Brad's grip. Hot pokers of pain shot up my arm. I gasped, but I managed to turn so I was facing Margit now. Brad's back was to her and he was glaring at me, but Margit instinctively realized the danger we were in.

She nodded and sank down behind the cash counter. All that was visible of her were a few tufts of gray hair. With luck, Brad wouldn't notice her presence.

"You've got it all wrong," I said to him. "Look, if you'd just calm down, I'll let you search my belongings. You'll see I don't have Eudora's nitro. We could go online and I can show you the other Zentangle designs. I did not try to draw a spider! In fact, I specifically cleared the patterns with her in advance."

"Don't worry," he snickered in a mean sort of

way. "I'll be happy to search your things thoroughly, before I turn you in. After I explain what you did, they'll be begging me to join the police force. I'll show them how a good cop handles a crime scene."

I laughed, but it sounded forced and pitiful even to my own ears. "You really think it's like some sort of secret club? Come on, Brad. You have to know better."

He pulled me close and bared his teeth in a snarl. "Shut up! You think you know about the police force? You don't! Jerks like that boyfriend of yours make me sick. And Vasquez? He's a total loser. They think they're better than me. But they aren't. I know how to run an investigation. I can put a creep behind bars as good as any of them!"

No way did I want to get into the car with Brad Oxemann. Detweiler and Robbie had drummed into my head the dangers of being removed from a crime scene. Once I was in the car with Oxemann, it would be nearly impossible for anyone to find me.

"How about if you just call the Felton police and have them come and arrest me? You'll still get credit for the collar. They're bound to be impressed by your detective skills."

Right.

"Sure they will. I'm taking you to the station myself." From inside his leather jacket, Brad pulled a gun. The weapon was big, black, gray, and lethal looking.

CHAPTER 64

"If we're going outside, I need my coat," I said, while looking down the barrel of a gun. "It's in the back."

"No way," said Brad, yanking me toward the front door. "You won't freeze to death in my van."

"Your van?"

"It's outside. In the parking lot. Now move it."

I shuffled toward the front door, knowing that when I opened it, the door minder would ring. But what good would that do? Clancy and Detective Vasquez would probably figure a customer had walked in. Or ignore the sound. So far, the two lovebirds hadn't stepped foot out of the back room.

Drat, drat, and double drat.

Margit was stuck behind the counter. For whatever reason, she was the only one who had heard Brad's threats. My abductor was pointing a gun at me. What else could I do, but follow his directions? I was flat out of options.

We stepped outside, and the front door closed behind us.

The wind had kicked up. The cold hit me like a

slap in the face. A snowflake landed on my cheek.

"What are you planning to say when you march me into the Felton police station?" I asked. "Won't this look a bit odd? You holding a gun on a pregnant woman?"

"Nah, we aren't going there right away. First we're stopping by my place. I have a video camera hooked up. After I get your confession, if you behave, we'll go to the police station."

This was getting worse by the minute.

There was an edge to his voice that caused a wave of panic to rise up inside me. The borders of my vision turned black—but I willed myself not to faint. What if I fell face first and hurt my baby? My baby! *What could I do to save us?* This man was a monster. Going home with him was not an option.

"Move it," said Brad, as I slowly picked my way through the small drifts of snow. The flakes were coming down as thick as feathers from a split pillow. They landed on my eyelashes and made me blink.

My baby had suddenly gone very still. Was he okay? I hoped so. Poor little thing. Would I make it out of this mess? What about Anya and Erik? How would they cope if I...

Died.

The thought caused my stomach to knot. It twisted so tightly, I couldn't breathe. My mouth flooded with bile. I tasted the burn of acid coming up in my throat.

"I'm going to be sick," I said, as we neared the white van. Brad had taken the empty space next to my BMW.

"Don't you even think about pulling tricks on me," said my captor.

I had no choice in the matter. My stomach knotted. A spasm swept through me.

The contents of my stomach splashed on the pavement next to the passenger side door of the van. The heat of the mess melted the newborn snow. My insides churned again and expelled everything so forcefully I thought I'd fall down. I put a hand on the side panel of the van to steady myself.

"Okay, that's disgusting," said Brad. "We'll go in on my side." He dragged me around the back of his van and shoved me against the driver's side door. I was crying now, whimpering with fear. But a new spasm of nausea doubled me over. I fought the urge to hurl while he fiddled with his keys.

To get his door unlocked, he had shifted his attention and as a consequence the muzzle of the gun was no longer pointed at me.

Looking down, trying to catch my breath, I saw the slick spot. The one I'd been doing my best to avoid. Brad had parked right beside the ice-covered dip in the pavement.

A breeze scattered the snow. The cold hit me so hard that I quaked violently. The icy patch winked in the sunlight—and gave me an idea. It wasn't much, but if I acted quickly, it might be all I needed.

A loud burp erupted from my rolling stomach. Instead of squelching it, I let it go full force.

Brad thought I was going to puke again. Instinctively, he jumped away from me and turned his head in disgust.

The diversion lasted only a fraction of a second, but that was all I needed. I took two quick steps backwards. My feet went into a skid. My legs scrambled in the air. I came down hard. My back hit the snow, knocking the wind out of me with a loud "oomph."

I started sliding fast. With a desperate jink to one side, I grabbed the rocker panel of the van. Using arms made strong from picking up Erik, I enhanced my trajectory. My entire body skidded along the ice. Heedless of the pain, I grabbed at the hot undercarriage. It stung but I hung on.

Brad threw himself toward me. His hands snatched at my feet. Bracing myself against the car's frame, I held on tightly. He tugged so hard one of my shoes came off and sent him sprawling. I pulled myself so that I was completely out of his reach, safe and sound, staring up at the under carriage of the van.

CHAPTER 65

Brad stomped around, cursing and muttering dark threats.

I shivered and tried to get my wits about me. It was actually warmer under the van than it had been standing beside it. The pavement beneath me was snow-covered. My body heat would quickly turn it to slush. Already I could feel moisture soaking into my clothes. My teeth chattered violently, but my major concern was for my little passenger. As though he read my thoughts, he kicked me under the ribs. I imagined him giving me two thumbs up and a great big grin of approval.

My back ached from where I'd hit the ground to start my little "oopsie" slide. But that didn't matter much. I was safe. My covered position would make it difficult, if not impossible, for Brad to shoot at me. First he would have to get down on his knees in the snow, and then he'd have to aim from that awkward position. He couldn't pull me out into the open because my were tucked under the car. At least for the moment, I was safe.

My heart pounded so loudly that I was sure he

could hear it, too. The *thump-thump-thump* almost drowned out the sound of Brad ranting and raving.

"Get out!" he yelled at me. "Come on!"

His hand waved around in the space between the van and the ground. His feet were inches from my face. I scooted further away from the opening.

If need be, I could stay under here all day.

A gust of wind sent a spit of snow up my pants leg.

Or not.

Surely Margit would have come out of hiding and dialed nine-one-one by now. I crossed my fingers.

"Either you get out from under there or—" Brad's threat was cut short.

"Police! Put your hands up!" Detective Vasquez shouted.

"No way!" Brad yelled back. "I've caught the killer! She's under my van! Come on, man. I'll give you partial credit for the collar!"

"Drop your gun," said Vasquez. "I mean it, pal. Do it or I'll shoot."

"Wait a minute! I'm not the bad guy here. This woman killed an old lady. I've got proof. All you need to do is—"

In the distance, a siren wailed.

Margit must have pressed the panic button, the one installed under the counter by the cash register. Bless her heart!

"Drop your gun," repeated Vasquez. "Do it now! You can hear the sirens. I've got back up coming."

"You're making a big mistake," said Brad.

"The biggest of your career."

"Really?" Vasquez answered back with a decided question in his voice. "I'm not the one who's about to be surrounded by angry cops."

How stupid would Brad be?

My shivering got worse. I tried to avoid the parts of the van that still radiated enough heat to burn me, but I also craved the warmth, any warmth, because I was now soaked to the skin. For the moment, I was safe, but soon I would have to tinkle. The pressure on my bladder was intensified by how cold I was.

The sirens had gone silent.

Did that mean back up wasn't coming?

Was it possible that Margit hadn't called the cops?

What was going on out there? It seemed like hours had passed since Vasquez had ordered Brad to drop his gun.

And then I heard a loud *bang*.

CHAPTER 66

The bang turned out to be a shot fired by Brad Oxemann.

Fortunately, Brad didn't have a good aim. Most people, in the heat of the moment, can't hit the broad side of a barn. Even seasoned cops shoot wide during gun battles. Of course, Brad was not a seasoned cop, and he wasn't nearly as smart as he thought he was. Nor was he much of a gunslinger. In fact, he was what Margit cheerfully called later, "A doofus."

Consequently, his bullet whizzed past Detective Vasquez's head and lodged in the wooden siding of our building.

Although Brad had failed to shoot the detective, he did manage to tick him off.

Mightily.

Later I learned, if Clancy hadn't thrown open the back door to see what was happening, Raoul Vasquez might have returned fire and shot a big old hole in Brad Oxemann's chest. Instead, the cop chose to head-butt Brad and knock the creep to the ground. Once he cuffed Brad and hauled him to his feet, the detective looked up to see

Clancy standing at his side. They exchanged a brief hug.

Cara reported all this to me. "It was one of those scenes right out of an old Western. The shoot-out occurs, the good guy escapes by the skin of his teeth, and the leading lady races out to throw her arms around her man. Margit and I couldn't help but giggle!"

I heard Clancy ask Vasquez, "Are you hurt?"

"Never better," Detective Vasquez said. "Although shooting this idiot would have made my day. You might want to help your friend."

"Hey! Hello? Is it safe to come out? Anyone? I'm freezing down here!"

"Kiki?" Clancy said, in a startled voice. "Where is she?"

"Under the van."

"Again?"

"What do you mean by *again*?" asked Detective Vasquez.

"Never mind." Clancy leaned down and casually asked, "Kiki? You plan on staying down there?"

"Nope. Just until it's all clear," I said, speaking to her upside-down face.

"Raoul, uh, Detective Vasquez has that turkey spread-eagle and bent over the hood of your car." Her hair was brushing against the snow.

"Tell him he better not scratch my paint."

"Right. Good to know you have your priorities straight." Her features were curiously slack. It's not time so much as gravity that is the great enemy of our looks. "Better yet, how about if you climb out and tell him yourself?"

"Give me a hand?"

She reached toward me. We locked fingers.

"One, two, THREE!" With a hearty pull, she freed me.

"Good deal," she said, as she helped me to my feet. "I thought we were going to have to invite the fire department to drop by again."

Vasquez tossed Clancy his keys and instructed her to pull a blanket from the back of the Escalade. Her teeth were chattering, too, as she wrapped me up. We sounded like a pair of castanets, clacking away.

"Go on." I pulled the blanket around me tightly. "Get back inside the store before you catch cold. I'm fine."

She frowned.

"I'm fine and the detective's busy. Now go!"

She made a fussy harrumphing sound and skedaddled back inside.

That left me patiently answering questions from the cops who arrived in our parking lot. Doors slammed. Feet crunched the snow. Walkie-talkies crackled. Lights rotated.

An army of law enforcement officials had shown up in response to Margit pushing the panic button. Later I learned that Clancy had also put in a call and that Detective Vasquez had requested back up as well. A nice looking young woman in uniform suggested that she call an ambulance to take me to the emergency room, but I told her no dice. I wasn't hurt. At least, not much. My backside was sore from the fall I'd taken. Bumps and bruises I could handle at home.

CHAPTER 67

After they shoved Brad Oxemann into the back of a police cruiser, Vasquez came over to talk to me. "Mrs. Lowenstein? I need you to come down to headquarters so someone can take your statement."

"No problem. Do you mind if I get my purse and phone? I'd like to call Detweiler. He's likely to have heard about this. Surely someone is monitoring the local scanners. I want him to know I'm all right."

Vasquez smiled at me. "I already called him. He'll meet us down at HQ. As for your purse, go ahead."

"Also, I might want to grab one of my Zentangle books."

"You planning on doing crafts while we sit around?" he asked, as he raised a dark eyebrow.

"Nope. I want to prove that a lot of the patterns look like spiders or spider webs, but that I did not purposefully draw anything that would have scared Eudora Field. In fact, I did everything I could to avoid upsetting her that way."

"You are welcome to grab your stuff, but I

hope you realize that our investigation into the death of Miss Field will be ongoing. Frankly, I don't give Brad Oxemann's theories any weight at all. But if it makes you feel better, I'll look at what you've got."

Two hours later, I was sitting in an interview room, using my Sakura Micron .05 pen to draw my favorite tangles, designs that Rick Roberts calls, "Comfort tangles," those patterns we instinctively return to when we're stressed. Detective Vasquez had made sure I was comfortable. He even found another blanket for me because my clothes were still wet. Another detective, Andy Milchberg, was dispatched to bring me a hot chocolate and walk me through the events of the afternoon.

Milchberg was a clean cut young man, who had proudly served our country as a Marine before becoming a cop. He had two kids, and a wife who loved scrapbooking. Of course, I wrote out a coupon to give to her.

"She's going to flip," he said, looking down at my business card. "Sandy will love this!"

As we talked, I completed two tiles, two pieces of Zentangle art. Milchberg was totally impressed, so I signed and dated one and gave it to him. In exchange, he bought me a second cup of hot chocolate. This one even had an extra squirt of vanilla in it!

Zentangle does calm people down, and I proved as much by getting drowsy as the questions dwindled to a natural conclusion.

"I need to leave you here for a bit," said Detective Milchberg. "Will you be okay?"

"Sure," I said, as I pulled one of the blankets up higher around my neck. Overhead, a florescent light buzzed like a drowsy bee. I took one last sip of hot cocoa, pushed the cup away, and rested my head on the cold laminate table top. The surface smelled of coffee, probably spilled in interviews gone by. My eyes didn't want to stay open. But if I fell asleep, I'd probably drool on the table.

Who cared?

I didn't.

Okay, I did.

The Felton police didn't know me. I decided that I really should be on my best behavior. Slobber would definitely damage my image as a businesswoman.

On the other hand, it *had* been a long afternoon, full of excitement that had culminated with a shot from Brad Oxemann's gun.

I was almost asleep when the door to the interview room flew open.

"Kiki? You okay?" Detweiler gathered me into his arms. The baby bump wasn't much of an impediment to his strong hug. "Babe? Talk to me!"

"I'm fine."

My little passenger kicked at the sound of his daddy's voice.

"Your son is fine, too," I said, sighing with happiness at the warmth of Detweiler's body. For awhile, I stayed there, feeling secure and loved.

Then he set me back down on the chair. "You sure? The Felton Police Chief is talking to Vasquez and Milchberg. They've got Oxemann in a cell. Maybe I should take you to the hospital.

You must have hit the pavement pretty hard."

"I'm a little sore, but I'm okay."

The extra chair scraped the floor as he dragged it close to mine. "Sweetie, I still can't believe this. Hiding under that creep's van? So smart of you."

"I didn't have much choice. You and Robbie have harped on the dangers of going quietly with a scumbag. At first, Oxemann said he was bringing me here. Then he told me he had a video camera set up at his apartment, and he was going to question me."

Detweiler's green eyes turned a dark emerald color. "You're kidding."

"No."

"I need to tell Vasquez about that. Hang on," and he ran out of the room.

This time I did fall asleep on the table top.

I only drooled just a little.

CHAPTER 68

Saturday, December 17...

By a unanimous decision of everyone else but me, I stayed home all day Saturday. Detweiler was honked off because I hadn't shared details about my first slip-and-slide adventure. No matter how often I explained that it hadn't been a big deal, he was put out.

Laurel assured me the store would be fine. Later she called to report that Rebekkah had come in to help. She also told me that Clancy's spa baskets had been a huge success.

That night Detweiler, Cara Mia and I went to the party at her family's restaurant while Brawny stayed home and made cookies with the kids. Clancy showed up on Detective Vasquez's arm. I don't remember ever seeing her look happier. Raoul's attentiveness put a glow on her face. He treated her like a queen. That was exactly the sort of ego boost that Clancy needed, because her husband had dumped her for a younger woman.

Actually, I couldn't imagine why. You'd have to search long and hard to find a woman more lovely than Clancy. In her aqua silk blouse and long black skirt, she looked as if she'd stepped from the pages of a fashion magazine. Since both she and Raoul have dark hair, they made a striking couple.

While Detweiler danced with Clancy, Raoul and I went into a huddle off by ourselves. "Your Zentangle book proved that there were a lot of patterns that might have upset Ms. Field, but nothing specific. We still haven't found her nitroglycerin tablets, and frankly, we don't have anything else to go on."

"What's going to happen to Brad?" I asked, as I watched Cara greet her former employees. She was wearing a stylish black dress with long sleeves and a neckline cut just low enough to show off her tan. I was wearing a jade green pair of satin pajamas. With a gold necklace and earrings, the jammies had been transformed into chic evening apparel.

"We have enough charges to keep him behind bars for quite a while. I'll let you know if anything changes. The fact he'd set up a camera and planned to interrogate you makes his situation worse. We found duct tape, and other, um, items. He wasn't planning to just ask you questions."

"Ugh." That revelation caused me to nearly drop my drink, a glass of tonic water mixed with pomegranate juice.

Early Sunday, the day after the party, I drove Cara Mia to the airport.

"I hate to see you go," I said, hugging her hard.

"When are you coming to Florida?"

"Soon," I promised and I meant it.

Later that day, Anya and Erik attended Laurel's Fantasy Jars class. The gifts they made were absolutely adorable! And I'm not saying that because I'm their mother. The other moms were equally impressed with the project.

Laurel was fast becoming a sort of big sister to my children. "Anytime Brawny needs a break, my boyfriend Joe and I would be happy to babysit," she told me. "I know that at thirteen Anya doesn't need a sitter, but..."

"But I'm not about to leave her and Erik alone in the house," I finished for her. "Thanks for the offer. I'll probably take you up on it. Brawny mentioned there are a few things that Lorraine might need help with back in California."

"Just so you know," said Laurel, lifting a lock of her blond hair off of her forehead, "we'd love to spend time with the kids. Even after the baby comes. It wouldn't be an imposition at all."

She blushed and added, "Joe and I think of it as a practice run. We want at least three kids."

I smiled at her. "And I hope you'll have them. You two would be wonderful parents!"

CHAPTER 69

The next week raced by. Our house was filled with wonderful smells as Brawny and the kids made a new type of Christmas cookie each day.

Even Monroe seemed to be in a good mood. Twice the people from St. Toby's fetched the donkey so they could rehearse their Christmas pageant. As a thank-you gesture, they gave us a special invitation with reserved seating.

"I don't want to go because Brittany Ladarov will be front and center," said Anya. "But I *do* want to go because it'll be the night before Christmas."

"I want to see Monroe," said Erik.

"Then I'll go," said Anya, taking his hand. "We can see him together okay?"

"Yup," said Erik.

Oops. My bad. Sheila had warned me I needed to quit substituting "yup" for "yes."

My mother-in-law had been very quiet since making a scene at the store. I'd hoped for an apology, but that wasn't really her style. The way I see it, if an apology will mend a broken relationship, or soothe hurt feelings, it's a small price to pay. My ego isn't so fragile that I need to protect it at all costs. But Sheila, she saw apologies as a sign of weakness. To my mind, it's the bigger person who'll say, "I'm sorry."

Strange, huh?

So things were a mite frosty when Sheila, Robbie, Detweiler and I showed up at the holiday event at CALA. My mother-in-law was in her element, since the staff at CALA usually fawns over her. I detected the slightest hint of slurring of her words, but she was sober enough to be presentable in public.

Hearing Erik sing a solo part in Jingle Bells was the highlight of the evening for all of us. Maggie told me that he was becoming more and more comfortable in the classroom. "I think having Anya nearby helps tremendously."

Anya certainly played her part of "proud older sister" to perfection. She scooped up Erik at the end of the event and introduced him to all of her classmates. They made a fuss over the adorable little boy. Unfortunately, not all of their parents were as open-minded.

One mother had the gall to ask, "What nationality is that boy?"

"He's a Martian," I said. "We had to apply for a special visa just to bring him into this galaxy. Oh, and I'm pregnant with an alien from Saturn. He'll be attending CALA right alongside your lovely offspring."

That shut her up.

CHAPTER 70

As we got closer and closer to Christmas, fewer and fewer customers dropped by the store. However, when Margit ran the numbers, we were well ahead of projected sales. Clearly we were going to make a nice profit. That gave me yet another reason to celebrate!

On Tuesday, we celebrated the eighth day of Hanukkah at the store by giving away "gold coins," which are really foil-wrapped chocolates, a substitute for *gelt*. We lit the last of the Hanukkah candles at home. Keeping with tradition that George and I had started, all of us gave each other books. The traditional paper kind.

I'd decided to have our store party run all day on Wednesday. That way we wouldn't have to compete with parties happening the last weekend before Christmas. As a special bonus, I planned to teach the Album in a Folder class several times, so people could easily schedule it on their busy calendars.

Every one of the Crafty Cuties signed up for the six o'clock class.

"*Ja*, and you should give them back Eudora's

things," Margit reminded me. "They are still here in the back room. We want to clear out everything that we can, so it will be easier to take an inventory in January."

I'd forgotten all about the bag with her things, so I thanked Margit for reminding me.

At five-thirty, our customers started showing up for the class. First to arrive was Bonnie Gossage, an attorney and long-time patron. She and I compared baby bumps. Since she was due two weeks after I was, she was a tad smaller than I. We had a good laugh about our expanding waistlines.

Five minutes before the start of the class, I handed Eudora's bag over to her sister, Ester.

"I can't even remember what might be here," she said. "But I'm sure I can use the supplies." Sitting down at our craft table, she dumped the contents of the bag. "I wonder how much paper is left in this notebook. It might not even be worth taking home."

As I watched, she flipped open the notebook to where Eudora had used a paperclip to mark her place.

Two huge squashed spiders were stuck to the page.

"Oh!" squealed Ester, jumping back and knocking over her chair.

"Those are fishing spiders," I said on closer inspection. "They live near water."

"Their bodies are nearly an inch long!"

"Yup. They look scary, but they're actually a boon to us. They eat mosquito larvae." Touching one of the legs with a pencil, I watched it break into pieces. That told me the arachnids had been dead a long time.

"So someone did scare Eudora!" said Ester. "My sister was murdered! But how?"

I stared down at the spiders. "I don't know. Could someone have put these into her notebook before she came to our class?"

"They must have," said Ester. "But that doesn't make sense. She came from home to the community center. Those are the only two places where she had her supplies."

The other Crafty Cuties had been watching our exchange. Marvela spoke up, "Don't forget her nitro was missing too. I know because that detective asked me if I'd seen her use it. We all knew she kept it in her bag."

"Her bag!" I said. "That's it!"

CHAPTER 71

"Let me get this straight," said Raoul Vasquez, as he pulled up a chair at the crafts table. "Ms. Field was on her way into the community center and Brad Oxemann did what?"

"He helped her. See, she had problems getting her scooter up the handicapped ramp and into the building. There was this ridge, and the scooter got stuck on it every time," explained Lois Singer.

"So Eudora would text-message Brad and tell him when she was arriving," said Ruby LeCuero. "He'd keep an eye out for her van. When she pulled up, he'd go and help her over the hump."

"But this particular time, her things fell out of her panniers, the leather pouches attached to her scooter," I said. "Remember, ladies? I saw it happen. She mentioned that they had dumped out right when we started the class."

Laurel nodded. "All the other women had their notebooks out and were ready to get to work. But she searched through the pockets and didn't find her notebook where it usually was."

"We all had to wait for her. When she didn't find it in the first pannier, she looked in the other one, and there it was," said Ester.

"Kiki was at the front of the room, ready to show us our new tangle, but she was waiting until Great Aunt Eudora found her notebook," said Caitlyn.

"As soon as Eudora found it, Kiki started the class," said Cecily Kelly. "We were all looking at Kiki when she opened her book."

I pointed to the paperclip. "She always kept a paperclip inside to mark a fresh page. I imagine that she flipped the book open and saw the dead spiders, just like Ester did earlier today."

Detective Vasquez nodded thoughtfully. "But what happened to her nitro?"

"Brad was a member of the Spanish club while Miss Field was the adviser back when he was in high school," said Laurel. "He probably knew her habit of using a paperclip, and I bet he also knew where she kept her nitro."

"That's right!" said Ester. "My sister has been using a scooter for more than ten years. She needed hip replacement surgery, but she wouldn't get it. Because of her dicey heart, she worried that she wouldn't come out of the anesthesia. As her hip got worse, she relied more and more on the motorized scooter to get around."

"Brad would have known about the paperclip, known about the nitro, and been in the right place to plant the dead spiders," I said. "We have means and opportunity."

Clancy slid a plate of cookies in front of me. "I'm happy to bring all of you drinks," she said. "Coffee? Tea?"

Raoul Vasquez smiled at her. "Coffee, black

and hot, please."

She tore her eyes away from him and took orders from our other guests. Laurel tapped her lower lip with a fingertip. Staring at the dead spiders, she seemed miles away in her thoughts. "I know why he did it. It's simple: He wanted to solve the murder."

She was right!

"He wanted to prove that the police force needed him. He told me so himself," I said.

"Framing Kiki would have been easy," said Caitlyn. Turning to me, she explained her thinking. "Remember how you always tossed your demo drawings into the recycling bin there in the room we used? He probably looked at them and realized he could make a case for how they resembled spiders."

"Of course!" I hopped up and ran into the back room. It took me a minute, but I came back with my previous lesson plans. A couple of those tangles started with lines that could have been construed as "spider-like," if you really pressed the point.

"All Zentangle patterns start simple," I explained to Raoul. "By adding one stroke of the pen after another, they take on their individualistic beauty."

He glanced over the handout sheet and the step-by-step breakdowns of the patterns. "I don't see it, but we have to remember that Brad also planned to interrogate you. That's probably how he planned to 'close' the case."

"There's one way to see if he's the killer or not," I said. "I bet if you get a search warrant for his vehicle, you'll find Eudora's bottle of nitroglycerin pills."

CHAPTER 72

"O come let us adore him!" Erik sang at the top of his lungs while swinging his hand, which was tightly holding onto Anya's. A couple of snowflakes fluttered down, blurring the golden glow of the spotlights trained on the Nativity Scene at St. Toby's. Our whole family was seated in the front row, next to parents of the pageant participants. Clancy and Raoul had declined the invitation at the last minute. I think they had something more intimate in mind.

Detweiler had made a crack about how we were Monroe's parents, and I thought the kids would never stop giggling. Our favorite donkey stood patiently behind Mary and Joseph as the couple stared down at the swaddled baby in the manger.

Actually, poor little Jesus looked as if he'd seen better days. From my vantage point, I could see a black scuff mark on his plastic head.

I knew the feeling.

Between finishing up my holiday shopping, wrapping gifts, working at the store, and answering questions about Eudora Field's murder,

I had a raging headache. Almost as if someone had kicked me in the head. Thinking of it, I put a hand to my temple. Was there a scuff mark there?

Oh, well.

At least Brad Oxemann was going to jail for a long, long time. The crime scene techs had quickly found Eudora's bottle of nitroglycerin stuffed between the owner's manual and a porn magazine in the glove compartment of Brad's car. That, plus his attempted abduction of a pregnant young mother—me!— and his obvious intent to do me bodily harm, did not make Brad a good candidate for rehabilitation. They discovered he had an entire arsenal of weapons, both legal and illegal. Raoul had reported all this to us, finishing his commentary with, "That creep can kiss his butt goodbye."

I was thinking about Eudora's murder as Detweiler hugged me tight. He bent low, planted a kiss by my ear, and whispered into my knitted cap, "This is what I've wanted my whole life, and I owe it all to you. Thank you for our family."

"Here I thought you were attending just because of the donkey," I whispered back.

That made us both laugh.

A woman behind us shot me a dirty look, but I gave her a smile in return. To my astonishment, her frown cracked and she actually smiled back. Such was the power of the season.

The music changed as the Three Wise Men entered the tableau. The beard on one of them hung crookedly from his chin, but who cared? Their sumptuous robes and shining crowns vividly contrasted with Mary's simple gown.

During the course of the pageant, Brittany Ladarov had managed to pull her neckline down farther and farther so she was now showing a bit of teenage cleavage.

There had been a gasp from her mother when Brittany had first made her appearance, walking demurely beside Monroe. She'd definitely overdone her blue eye shadow and liner, giving the wholesome Virgin a decidedly tawdry look.

"She did not leave the house looking like that!" Nita Ladarov said to the woman sitting next to her.

Even the priest blinked in surprise at Brittany's bee-stung lips, which had been painted a holly berry bright red.

"I am sooo not surprised." Anya turned to me and rolled her eyes.

"Behold! Unto us a savior is born!" said a girl dressed as an angel. With a sweep of her hand, she pointed at the doll with the scuffed up face.

Brittany, not one to miss a cue, leaned down to coo over the Christ Child.

In what must have been an unscripted moment, Brittany took her role too far. She reached into the manger and picked up Baby Jesus. I opened my mouth to shout a warning. Time slowed to a crawl. The faces around me stared straight ahead in rapturous adoration at the Mother and Child.

I was focused on Monroe.

It was almost as if I could read his mind. The donkey took one glance at the swaddling clothes. A single thought flashed through his head: Diaper!

I saw Monroe drop his head.

Anya shouted, "No!"

In an overly dramatic gesture, Brittany turned her eyes toward heaven.

Monroe tucked his chin.

"Stop!" yelled Detweiler.

Monroe took aim.

"Please, please, don't!" I said, with all the urgency I could muster.

Monroe flicked his muzzle forward, executing a perfect head butt.

"There he goes!" said Erik, pointing a finger at the donkey-propelled missile.

And Baby Jesus went soaring up, up, up and over our heads.

~ The End ~

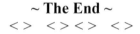

TWELVE DAYS OF CHRISTMAS PROJECTS

Tuesday-Margit-Carolers
Wednesday-Kiki-Icosahedrons
Thursday-Brawny-Crocheted Necklace
Friday-Laurel-Snowman Luminaria
Saturday-Clancy-Spa Gift Basket
Sunday-Laurel-Fantasy Jars
Monday-Rebekkah-Dodie's Turtles and Margit-Gingerbread Man
Tuesday-Brawny-Quilted Glasses Case
Wednesday-Kiki-Album in a Folder
Thursday-Margit-Dollhouse Notebook
Friday-Clancy-MiniBook Earrings
Saturday-Kiki-Book Garden
< >   < > < >   < >

Remember, you can download your free copy of a tutorial for all these projects by sending an email to **HHHBonus@JoannaSlan.com** If you have any questions or problems with the download, contact Joanna's assistant, Sally Lippert at **SALFL27@att.net** We'll also add you to Joanna's newsletter list at no charge!

Kiki's Story Continues in the Next Book in the Series
Shotgun, Wedding, Bells (Book #11)
Here's the link—
http://www.amazon.com/Shotgun-Wedding-Lowenstein-Scrap-N-Craft-Mystery-ebook/dp/B00SURBH7A/ref=sr_1_1?s=books&ie=UTF8&qid=1428335264&sr=1-1&keywords=shotgun%2C+wedding%2C+bells

Or use this shortened version –
http://tinyurl.com/ShotWedBells

A NOTE FROM THE AUTHOR—

If you enjoyed this book, we hope you'll consider "liking" us on Facebook
http://tinyurl.com/JCSlan
and/or adding a review on Amazon
http://tinyurl.com/JoannaSlan
or Goodreads. We also hope you'll tell a friend! (Or two or three!) Your opinion matters to me, and it will help other readers find my work.

Don't forget our special gift to you. If you send an email to **HHHBonus@JoannaSlan.com**,

we'll automatically send you a pdf with the tutorials for Kiki's Christmas Projects, and a few extra goodies. If you have any problems with the download, you can always email Sally Lippert, my assistant, at **SALFL27@att.net**

Also, we've made every attempt to catch any mistakes in this piece, but they do happen. (Type lice crawl into the computer and rearrange letters when we aren't looking. Honest!) So if you see something that's wrong, please email my assistant Sally Lippert at **SALFL27@att.net**

She'll find a way to break it to me gently.

All best from your friend,

Joanna

P.S. I hope you enjoy the bonus read that follows. It's the beginning of **Tear Down and Die,** the first book in a new series featuring one of Kiki's friends, Cara Mia Delgatto. Reviewers on Amazon are giving it 4.8 stars out of 5.

Turn the page for your Free Bonus Excerpt

TEAR DOWN AND DIE
A Cara Mia Delgatto Mystery
(Book #1)
~ 4.8 stars out of 5 stars on Amazon ~
By Joanna Campbell Slan

PROLOGUE

Late August…
St. Louis, Missouri

As if he were looking out into the future, the light faded in Sven's brown eyes, and his weight settled in my arms. A sob burst from my chest, as I whispered, "He's gone, isn't he?"

The vet, a grizzled man near retirement age who had a habit of clicking his dentures, pressed the stethoscope to my dog's chest. After what seemed like an eternity, he nodded.

"I killed my dog," I said to my friend Kiki, as her fingers gripped my shoulder. "I killed him!"

With surprising strength, she grabbed me and turned me so that we faced each other. "You did not kill him. He's been having seizures for the past eight hours. You released him, Cara Mia. You gave him peace!"

I threw my arms around her neck and cried. I choked and sputtered and moaned and keened while all the sadness of the past year heaved up inside me and overflowed onto the shoulder of my friend. Kiki Lowenstein simply held me, patting my back, making soothing sounds.

When I was nearly cried out, the vet asked, "Do you want to take your pet?"

Kiki's fiancé, Detective Chad Detweiler made a move to bundle Sven in a blanket, but I said,

"No. Please cremate him. I plan to leave the area. I want Sven to go with me."

The rest of the visit was a blur. The staff murmured their condolences as we walked through the office. Other clients looked away. They understood instinctively what had happened. The tall detective opened the door for us, and we climbed into Detweiler's big police cruiser. Kiki and I sat in the back seats so she could hold me. We'd made quite a fuss on our arrival. Detweiler had used his flashing lights to speed us through the city traffic as I watched Sven convulsing on my lap. Silently, I thanked my lucky stars for having friends who dropped everything to come to my aid at a moment's notice. Leaving St. Louis would be hard, but it was time. My parents were both gone, having died within six months of each other, and my son was off to college.

Now this.

"I am never, ever going to own another dog," I said. "Ever."

For a long portion of the ride, Kiki said nothing. She put her arm around my shoulders and let me cry, leaking tears now rather than sobbing.

When we pulled up to my house, she walked me inside while Detweiler waited for her in his car. I appreciated how he gave us a bit of privacy. After she got me settled on my sofa and made me a cup of peppermint tea, Kiki sank down next to me and said, "Now you listen to me, Cara Mia, and you listen good. Of course you'll get another dog. Of course you'll love again. I know you and I know that you believe in second chances. We both do. That's what makes life worth living. And if you forget how important they are, if you start to doubt that they are worth the heartache, remember this—"

She pressed my fingertips to her belly so I could feel her baby kick. "Second chances," she said. "That's what life's all about. Don't you ever doubt it."

CHAPTER 1

Early September...

Sometimes you need to go backwards to move forwards. Especially when you doubt yourself and don't know what to do next. All my packing was done. Boxes that would go into storage formed an untidy wall around me.

"Where you moving to?" asked one of the men from the van lines, as he flicked the butt of a Camel cigarette onto my lawn. Except it wasn't my lawn. Not anymore. So why worry?

"I haven't decided yet."

That pretty much summed up my life. I was at a crossroads, a spot on the map between emptiness and confusion—and I didn't know which way to turn. Watching the workers load up my stuff only made me feel more unsettled. I signed the paperwork for the movers, hopped in my car, the black Camry I've named Black Beauty and drove to a familiar parking lot.

"Cara Mia Delgatto! I've been expecting you." Kiki stood at the back door of her scrapbook and crafting store, Time in a Bottle. A red dog leash connected her to her rescue pup, Gracie, a harlequin Great Dane.

"Let me guess. You were on your way to take this lovely dog for a potty break." I reached down and patted the floppy ears on the black and white giant.

"Uh-huh. Care to come with? You can tell me how you've been."

We hadn't gotten halfway around the block when I broke down and started crying uncontrollably. Kiki and I perched on a low concrete block retaining wall so I could sob while Gracie sniffed and peed. Kiki put her arm around me, and I wet her shoulder with tears while she patted my back and murmured, "Get it all out, Cara. You'll feel better."

When I'd cried me a river (the Mississippi, I'd guess from the muddy look of it), we started back to the shop. Once inside, Kiki put Gracie in the doggie playpen and grabbed a Diet Dr Pepper for me and a bottle of water for her.

"It's done. Everything's going into storage. I couldn't stand being in that big house night after night by myself," I said. "I don't want to see the restaurant again, either. It doesn't matter whether it's called Cara Mia's or not. That was our place, our family place. Now that Mom and Dad have passed away, and Tommy's left for school, there's nothing to keep me here in St. Louis. Besides, winter is coming and I've always hated cold weather."

"Time to make a new plan and move on down the highway." Kiki smiled at me, her curls framing her round face. One hand rested protectively on her belly.

"But I'll be leaving so much behind."

"Yes, and you have your whole life ahead of you. Come on back to the store. I have a little gift for you."

When I was seated at her work table, she handed me a gift bag filled with tissue paper. I reached inside and pulled out a memory album of my years in St. Louis.

"This is just grand." I paged through the album. "I could never have done anything like this."

"We all save our memories in different ways. You are just as sentimental as I am, Cara. Look at you! I bet those are Tommy's old jeans you're wearing, right? Your son grew out of them and now they're yours."

"That's right. At the restaurant, I always had to wear a little black dress, so in my free time, I like dressing down. My belt was once my father's, but I had it shortened to fit. These rings on my right hand are my mother's engagement and wedding rings."

"May I remind you of all the redecorating you did at the restaurant, and how you came in under budget?" Kiki grinned. "In addition, you always smell like sandalwood. Is there a memory associated with that?"

"Sandalwood brings back good memories of summers in Florida. My parents used to rent an apartment above an antique store called The Treasure Chest. The owner stocked the rental with bars of sandalwood soap."

As she had predicted, that long crying jag had been cathartic. With my gift under my arm, we walked to Kiki's car. She reached in and handed me a heavy shopping bag.

"Another gift?" I squealed.

"There's a surprise for you to enjoy on the road so you'll think of me."

"Like I could ever forget you!" I took the gift and thanked her.

With her hands on my shoulders, Kiki looked at me with moist eyes. "I expect you to stay in touch."

Nodding, but too choked up to respond, I turned and walked to my car.

I waved once more, pulled out of the parking lot and tried not to look back. The hardest part of my journey was just ahead, as I'd have to drive past the Arch, that magnificent silver rainbow in the sky. It had always been a talisman, a welcome mat.

But this time, it seemed to wave goodbye.

~ To Be Continued ~

Purchase your copy of *Tear Down and Die* today at
http://www.amazon.com/Tear-Down-Cara-Delgatto-Mystery/dp/1495942457/ref=sr_1_1?ie=UTF8&q
id=1426253585&sr=8-
1&keywords=tear+down+and+die

or use this shorter link
http://tinyurl.com/TearDD

ABOUT THE AUTHOR

Joanna Campbell Slan started storytelling—and winning awards for her writing—at an early age. Today she's the author of eleven non-fiction books; a mystery series featuring Kiki Lowenstein, a spunky single mom who loves to scrapbook; a series featuring Charlotte Brontë's classic heroine, Jane Eyre, as an amateur sleuth; and a new series featuring Cara Mia Delgatto, an entrepreneur who specializes in second chances.

Joanna's first novel—***Paper, Scissors, Death*** (Book #1 in the Scrap-n-Craft Mystery Series featuring Kiki Lowenstein)—was a 2009 Agatha Award finalist. This series has been praised by the *Library Journal* as "topically relevant and chock-full of side stories." *Publisher's Weekly* calls them, "a cut above the usual craft-themed cozy."

RT Book Reviews has said that Kiki Lowenstein is "our best friend, our next-door neighbor and ourselves with just a touch of the outrageous."

Last year, Joanna won the coveted Daphne du Maurier Award of Excellence for Historical Romantic Mystery Suspense. She's also won the Silver Anvil Award for her written contributions to FarmAid.

Sharing Ideas Magazine has named Joanna "one of the top 25 motivational speakers in the world." She frequently appears before groups of all sizes to talk about writing, the creative lifestyle, and her successes.

Joanna is a prolific reader and writer. She's worn the letters off of four keyboards in her quest to keep telling stories that touch hearts and open minds. She lives with her husband David and their Havanese puppy, Jax, on Jupiter Island in Florida.

STAY IN TOUCH WITH US!

For a complete list of all Joanna's books and short stories, go to
http://tinyurl.com/JoannaSlan

To stay on top of all Joanna's offerings, join her mailing list, which is on her website at
www.JoannaSlan.com

To be part of Joanna's community, join her on Facebook at
www.Facebook.com/JoannaCampbellSlan

For craft tips, recipes, writing tips, and serialized short stories, follow Joanna at
www.JoannaSlan.blogspot.com

Join Joanna on Pinterest where you can see photos of her projects and memes from her books. The address is **www.Pinterest.com/JoannaSlan**

For quick updates, follow her tweets at
www.twitter.com/JoannaSlan

Contact Joanna by emailing her assistant, Sally Lippert, at **SALFL27@att.net** or you can write to her at **Joanna Campbell Slan, 9307 SE Olympus Street, Hobe Sound, FL 33455.**

Made in the USA
Middletown, DE
02 December 2015